THE WINDOW

Dave Cole

DANCING LEMUR PRESS, L.L.C.
Pikeville, North Carolina
www.dancinglemurpress.com

Published by Dancing Lemur Press, L.L.C.
P.O. Box 383, Pikeville, North Carolina, 27863-0383
www.dancinglemurpress.com

ISBN 9781939844767

Printed in the United States of America

Cover design by C.R.W.

Library of Congress Cataloging-in-Publication Data

Names: Cole, David, 1957- author.
Title: The window / Dave Cole.
Description: Pikeville, North Carolina : Dancing Lemur Press, L.L.C.,
    [2021] | Audience: Ages 13-18. | Audience: Grades 10-12. |
Summary:
    Brian Bingham enjoys looking through the mysterious attic window
that
    provides him with answers to upcoming tests and a glimpse of the
future,
    but after it accurately foretells his best friend's brutal death, Brian
    recognizes the threat the window poses to himself and those he
loves.
Identifiers: LCCN 2020027405 (print) | LCCN 2020027406 (ebook) |
ISBN
    9781939844767 (trade paperback) | ISBN 9781939844774 (ebook)
Subjects: CYAC: Future, The--Fiction. | Death--Fiction. | Best
    friends--Fiction. | Friendship--Fiction. | Dating (Social
    customs)--Fiction. | Family problems--Fiction.
Classification: LCC PZ7.1.C64278 Wi 2021 (print) | LCC
PZ7.1.C64278
    (ebook) | DDC [Fic]--dc23
LC record available at https://lccn.loc.gov/2020027405
LC ebook record available at https://lccn.loc.gov/2020027406

To Harold and Mildred, the Nutts in our family tree.

I was fifteen when I saw my best friend die. Although, if I think about it, I was fourteen when I saw him die the *first* time. Time had a way of confusing me that year. Ever since I've looked at past and present with a jaundiced eye. What is now and what is then? The one thing I'm certain about is that the worst year of my life started on December 16th, even though the bad stuff didn't happen until the next year. I'm certain of the date, because that's when I discovered the window.

December 16

On a normal year, our house would have been decorated from the basement to the roof, inside and out, by the end of Thanksgiving weekend. My mom lives for Christmas. She has special decorations for each room, festive lights for every window, and the whole house smells of pine, peppermint, and chocolate chip cookies fresh from the oven. Christmas music plays from morning until well after the outside lights have been illuminated. Her favorite songs are the religious ones or the classics like Bing Crosby's *White Christmas*, but she will sing along with anything with a hint of a Christmas connection.

But this isn't a normal year. It's already halfway through December and we still haven't bought a tree. Not a single decoration is up. Stockings aren't hung by the chimney with care, and I'm worried. I'm well past the age of believing in Santa Claus, but without a tree and without stockings, where are the presents supposed to go?

So, I'm overjoyed when she asks me to bring down the decorations.

"Brian, can you do me a favor and bring down the Christmas stuff from the attic?"

I drop my Xbox controller without even bothering to pause my game. My character will be dead before I even make it out of the living room, but I don't care. Christmas is finally coming!

"What do you need?" I yell, already climbing the stairs to the second floor of the house.

"Oh, anything you can find will be fine," she says. Her heart isn't in it, but I am confident the first couple of boxes of decorations will put her in the mood.

I jump, but I'm not quite able to reach the short rope that's used to pull the attic steps down from the ceiling. I give it one more shot for good measure, but I'm a few inches shy of the mark.

I'll be able to grab it by next year.

In the meantime, the chair from my desk gives me all the height I need to tug the ladder down. I scamper up the flimsy steps and poke my head into the attic.

I'll be honest. The attic used to scare the crap out of me when I was younger, and "younger" was last year when my mom asked me to help bring down the decorations. I had been afraid to go into the dark, dusty room full of nooks and crannies formed by the roofline. It was nothing short of terrifying to tiptoe over the creaking floorboards while blindly reaching for the string to turn on the single bulb hanging from the ceiling. Even the light didn't help much. The dim light turned stacks of boxes into fearsome shapes that shifted in the moving shadows created by the swaying bulb.

Today, though, the room feels a lot less frightening. At first, I think it's because I'm a year older, but that isn't it. The difference is the attic isn't dark. Even without pulling the string for the dusty lightbulb, the room is full of light. In the comforting glow, there are no monsters hiding in the nooks, just stacks of boxes, forgotten toys, and old pieces of furniture. In one corner is my old nightstand, with its blue, chipped Formica top and the small drawer missing its handle. I climb into the attic and seek out the source of light. I have to push a few stacks of boxes to one side and wrestle an old cupboard out of the way before I finally see it—a window.

It's octagonal, lined with beautiful woodwork that in no way matches the unfinished look of the attic with its plywood walls, but the window looks as though it belongs. A thin layer of dust covers everything in the room, but the woodwork surrounding the window gleams as if it has recently been buffed. I inhale deeply, half-expecting to smell the lemony scent of furniture polish lingering in the air.

Seeing a window that I swear wasn't there on my last trip to the attic is surprising enough, but it's what I see through the window that takes my breath away. The front yard is covered in snow! And not one of those dustings we get sometimes, where you can see the grass poking through the white and you know it will melt in the afternoon heat. No, this is real snow, at least six inches deep. It covers the street and hangs heavily from the trees, transforming the yard into a picture of white. The street hasn't been plowed yet, and there are no signs of people. The only blemish in the perfect coating of white is a set of tiny animal tracks leading from the evergreen to the base of the big elm tree in our yard—a squirrel, likely. The snow clinging to the tree branches cause the boughs to sag under the weight. Heavy snow is the best, not great for sledding but perfect for building a snowman with my sister or a snow fort for protection against a barrage of snowballs from the Allen twins next door.

The sky is a brilliant cobalt blue, that color no one can capture in a painting or photograph. It's the kind of winter day where everything is in complete focus. Every snow-covered twig stands out in stark detail. The wind pushes a piece of colorful wrapping paper up against the *Slow—Children* sign that marks the property line between our yard and Mr. Crowley's. The sign is an ongoing joke between JK, my best friend, and me. When he first saw it, he asked me if it meant drivers should slow down because there are children or if the neighborhood was populated with children who are "slow." Politically incorrect jokes about me riding the short bus invariably followed.

My focus is so clear I can tell it's Santa Claus wrapping paper pushed up against the sign, with the old fat guy in red smiling broadly in front of his sleigh and smoke rising from a pipe gripped firmly in one hand. The paper has a rip down one side, as if it had been torn quickly to get to the present lying beneath the colorful veneer. A piece of transparent tape hangs off one side, flapping in the breeze.

"You coming down, Brian?" my mom calls up from downstairs.

"Yeah, I'll be down in a minute."

I tear myself away from the window and gather up a handful of boxes labeled "Christmas decorations." I make sure to check that the box holding the stockings—plain ones for my parents and the cross-stitch ones my mom had made for my sister and me when we were born—are at the top of the stack. Before making my way to the stairs, I steal one last look out the window.

The snow is gone.

I press my nose to the window and stare out at the brown winter grass, no longer hidden under a blanket of white. The brilliant azure sky is now a dark smear of gray. I rapidly open and close my eyes, somehow trying to blink the snow back into existence. I want to think I had imagined the whole thing, but the vision had been so clear there was no way I created it in my mind.

I make at least a dozen trips up and down the attic steps over the next two hours—I was right that my mom got more into the Christmas spirit with each box of decorations I brought down—but the view out of the window doesn't change. The grass remains yellow-brown, the sky ash gray. There isn't a trace of snow anywhere. I check the window on each visit to the attic, but I don't see the snow again.

I put the strange vision out of my head as I release the attic stairs to ascend back into the ceiling. I smile as my mom sings off-key but enthusiastically to a Kelly Clarkson Christmas CD. I take a sniff, hoping to smell chocolate chip cookies baking. Not yet, but it won't be long.

December 25

The smell of coffee brewing wakes me from a sound slumber. I look sleepy-eyed at my cell phone on the nightstand for the time—7:45. I suffer a moment of panic, thinking I missed the school bus, before remembering it's the middle of winter break and I can sleep in as long as I want. I sink back into my pillow with a smile on my face after realizing I'm facing a day of no homework, no tests, and no papers due on the Emancipation Proclamation or the Louisiana Purchase.

I wonder if teachers are lying back with the same smile?

The smell of coffee grows stronger as my mom pokes her head into my room. The pleasant scent mixes with the nasty odor of her first or second or even third cigarette of the morning. She's smoking a lot more these days. My dad has been a two-pack-a-day guy since he was fifteen, but mom used to limit herself to five or ten cigarettes a day. She's up to a pack or a pack and a half now.

"Are you thinking about staying in bed all day?" she asks with a smile. "Because I can return your presents if you're not interested in opening them."

"Ten more minutes, Mom. I need my beauty sleep."

"C'mon, Brian." My littler sister's head appears in the doorway. "We need to see what Santa brought us!"

Becky is seven years younger than me. She's

at the age where she's questioning the existence of Santa Claus but is willing to believe just in case.

I roll over and pretend to go back to sleep, loud snores and all.

"C'mon, Brian," she pleads.

"Do you need help in here?" my dad's booming voice calls from the hallway.

"Yeah, Brian won't get out of bed," Becky says.

"Well, we'll have to see what we can do about that," he says. "It might be time to turn on the old tickle machine."

Becky giggles. The tickle machine is my dad's specialty. It doesn't matter how bad a day you are having. The tickle machine always makes things better.

I pull my blanket up over my head in a vain attempt to ward off the attack. My dad's heavy footsteps come toward the bed and stop when he reaches the edge.

"Hmm, where did he go?" he asks in mock confusion.

"He's under the covers, Daddy!"

I try to cover my sides, but my dad's probing fingers manage to find all the tickle spots he knows are my biggest weakness. I squirm, but it's no use. There is no known defense against the tickle machine.

"I give! I give!" I laugh. "I'm getting up!"

"The tickle machine always wins, doesn't it, Becky?" My dad winks, eliciting more giggles from her.

"Five minutes," my mom threatens, "or your presents get tossed out in the yard."

"Can I have them, Mom?" Becky asks.

"No, but you can have your own visit from the tickle machine," my dad replies.

Becky squeals and runs from the room and down the stairs.

"Don't you dare peek at those presents," my mom calls. "You can go into the kitchen and no farther!"

I grab a sweatshirt to throw on over my T-shirt and pajama pants. I pull a pair of socks from my dresser, and then I lift the pleated shades to look outside, squinting against the brightness. The socks drop from my hands when I see the snow.

It is exactly as I had pictured it from the attic window more than a week ago. Six inches of snow under a brilliant blue sky. The unplowed street with no signs of human activity. Without looking, I know there will be a tiny trail of squirrel prints leading to the elm tree, and there they are. I look to the *Slow— Children* sign at the edge of our yard, and there's the wrapping paper. Santa Claus and his sleigh, with the strip of tape bobbing in the breeze.

"You coming down, Brian?" my mom calls from the base of the stairs.

The words hit me like a shock. *Hadn't she said those same words while I looked at this same snow in the attic?*

"Yeah, I'm on my way," I reply in a voice that is steady, even though my heart pounds in my chest.

Apart from the snow, Christmas day feels normal. After we open our presents, we have a big family breakfast with eggs, bacon, and French toast swimming in a sea of maple syrup. Mom gets her fill of Christmas carols. Becky giggles while she dresses and undresses her new dolls. Dad even appears relaxed for a change, settling back into his overstuffed chair in the family room to read the new book he received from my mom, a thick tome on Alexander Hamilton. The smell of the roasting turkey with all the fixings fills the house. Most important of all, the tenseness that usually permeates the house is put aside for the day.

In the afternoon, JK pounds on the front door.

He is covered in clumps of snow and looks like the Michelin Man in his thick layers of winter wear.

"What the heck happened to you?" I ask as he stomps snow from his boots onto the front porch.

"Had an accident over on Coachlight," he replies. "I forgot about that big hole in the sidewalk and did a face plant. Luckily, the snow is soft. It would be a real shame to spoil this pretty face."

"Come on in and get warmed up." I stand to one side to allow him entry.

"No, you come out. The snow is perfect. Wait, are you in your freaking jammies? Dude, it's the middle of the afternoon."

"Hey, I'm chilling and enjoying the day off."

"Well, if you want some chilling, get your butt out here. The guys next door are already working on a fort. I'll get started on ours while you get dressed."

We've built a three-foot-tall wall facing the Allen's yard and are adding another foot to the top when the first snowball catches JK in the shoulder. I don't know if it was Dustin or Justin who fired the first shot. I have trouble enough telling the Allen twins apart under normal conditions and didn't even bother to try with their heads covered in ski masks.

JK and I scoop balls of snow and return fire. For the next hour we run and duck and throw, fighting off several attempts by the older boys to overrun our position. My cheeks are bright red from the cold and a couple of well-placed snowballs that found their mark. I can barely feel my fingers because I've traded the warmth of my gloves for the better accuracy of throwing bare-handed. The pristine white blanket of snow in the front yard looks like a war zone.

"Brian, it's time for dinner!" my sister calls from inside the front door.

"Thanks, Becky," I call back, raising my hands in a truce to the Allen twins. That gets a new barrage of snowballs thrown in our direction, so JK and I make a run for the safety of the porch.

"Cowards!" they yell after us.

JK raises the back of his hand in their direction. I'm pretty sure I can guess what gesture he's making inside the mitten.

We knock as much snow off each other as we can before entering the house, but we trail quite a bit of it inside. My mom had put towels on the floor for us in the foyer, so we take off our boots and drop our coats and hats on them. I rub my hands together to try to generate feeling back into my fingers.

"Merry Christmas, JK," my mom says as she pokes her head around the corner.

"Merry Christmas, Mrs. B."

"Can you stay for dinner?"

"The Wilsons are eating at six," he replies.

The Wilsons are JK's foster family. I've lost track of how many families he's gone through in the eight years I've known him. The Wilsons might be number seven. The Wilsons are a lot older than my parents, with three grown children of their own. They are nice enough, but there is a certain coolness to them. JK told me he didn't think they would foster him for more than a year, so he'll probably be uprooted again before we hit tenth grade. At eighteen, he will be on his own, and I worry about what that will mean for him.

"It's four o'clock," I counter. "You've got plenty of time to get in a good snack before dinner."

JK smiles. He always says he loves my mom's cooking, but it's more that he feels like we are his real family. And you should always be with family at Christmas.

"Yeah, I guess a snack wouldn't kill me." He grins. "Thanks, Mrs. B."

After dinner, we lounge in my room. I have a

present for JK, but I hold off on giving it to him. It isn't because I don't want him to have it. Nothing can be further from the truth. I'm worried about how he might feel if he doesn't have a present for me.

"Merry Christmas, man." JK surprises me by pulling a crumpled present from the pocket of his hoodie. The small package is inexpertly wrapped, with too much paper on one side and not quite enough on the other, and there is enough tape to secure a package four times its size. It doesn't matter, though.

"Hold on, I've got something for you, too." I tug my sock drawer open and extract a wooden box. "I didn't wrap it because...well, because I can't wrap any better than you can."

JK laughs, and we exchange presents. I let him open first because I want to see his face when he sees what's inside the box. He opens the lid slowly, and the hinges emit a tiny creak. He lets out a yell as he reaches inside and grabs the wand.

"Kingsley Shacklebolt!"

My parents had taken me to the *Wizarding World of Harry Potter* at Universal Studios over the summer. I'd saved my lawn mowing money to buy a wand and was deciding between Harry Potter (11" holly, phoenix feather core) or Remus Lupin (10 ¼" cypress, unicorn hair core) when I saw this wand. I knew immediately it was the one JK would have chosen if he were with me. Kingsley Shacklebolt was one of the few black characters in the Harry Potter movies and was, in the studied opinion of JK, "one bad ass dude." I bought the wand on the spot and kept it hidden away in my sock drawer, waiting for the right moment to give it to him.

Now my friend swishes the wand from side to side, with a broad smile on his face.

"I was already about as cool as cool can be, but you know what this makes me, don't you?"

"Yeah, one bad ass dude."

"You got that right."

He stares at the wand reverently and then down at the floor. He's fighting back tears.

Overall, he's had a tough fourteen years. His foster parents are okay, but they will never be his real folks. His dad left before he was even born. His mom tried to raise him alone, but life hadn't worked out for her; she cut and ran when JK was four. All he remembers about her is that she'd had a big belly laugh. He's been in foster care ever since, never more than a year with a single family. No takers on adoption, so he's given up on it ever happening.

"Your turn, man." JK nods at my gift.

He watches as I tear into the wrapping paper, struggling to get through the layers of tape. Finally, I pull out a crumpled sheet of paper.

"I hope this is the answer key for the next history test."

"Trust me. It's better."

I unfold the paper in anticipation of one of JK's jokes. What I see instead is life changing for a fourteen-year-old boy. In JK's neat script is a note sent to—and more importantly, returned from—Charlotte O'Mara.

Charlotte,

My somewhat dorky friend Brian Bingham is interested in your thoughts on him:

☐ *He's hot!*

☑ *He's a little dorky, but cute*

☐ *Who is Brian Bingham?*

I am currently:

☐ *Available but not interested in someone who looks like that*

☐ *Secretly married to a Russian agent*

☑ *Available*

I might be interested in:

16

☐ *Seeing him thrown out of school*
☐ *Finding out who he is*
☑ *Going out with him*

A wave of emotions passes over me.

First, I am mortified. How could my best friend do this to me?

Second, I am pissed off. Seriously, how could my best friend do this to me?

Third, I am thrilled. Charlotte might be interested in going out with me?

The final emotion is pure terror. How could someone like me ask out someone like Charlotte? That leads me back to pissed off again. How could my best friend do this to me?

JK looks on anxiously, watching my face as I process all these emotions over the course of a few seconds. My face must have ended up on thrilled because he breaks out into a grin.

"Told you it was better than answers to a stupid test."

"I cannot believe you gave this to her."

"Well, believe it, buddy."

"And those checkmarks are hers?"

"Every last one of them."

"So, what do I do?" My voice shakes.

"Personally, I'd get her on the phone and let her know you have a much better option for her. A guy with the face of an angel and the body of a Greek statue. A taller, much better-looking version of you with an actual sense of humor."

"And who would that be?"

"Me, dude! I'm talking about me," JK says in a tone of righteous indignation.

I laugh, and then grow quiet.

"Thanks, man. I appreciate it, although this could have turned out so, so badly."

"Knowing you, it still might." He smiles.

"And what if it does?"

"Well, you know what they say, right?"

"You aren't going to feed me crap about when life closes a door it opens a window, are you?"

"No way. When life closes a door, open it back up. You know that's how a door works, right?"

I laugh. JK always has a line for everything.

"Seriously, man, this could have gone so wrong."

"I had a plan in case she checked the wrong boxes."

"You did?"

"Yeah, it involved you moving out of the state, leaving me to move in for myself."

I scowl. "And what if she decided I was the one she wanted?"

"Then she would have been devastated you moved, and I would have been forced to swoop in to console her." He grins. "Different path. Same result. The bad ass dude gets the girl." He swishes his new wand in emphasis.

An hour later, JK has his winter clothes back on, apart from his mittens, which are stuffed into his coat pockets. His new wand is held securely in one hand so he can brandish it in case dementors cross his path on the way home.

He gives it another practice swish. "Thanks, Brian. This is my best present ever."

"Glad you like it, JK. Your present is even better."

"That goes without saying."

"Too late. I already said it."

JK raises an eyebrow at my lame joke. "But it's totally wasted if you don't grow a pair and ask her out."

I start to laugh but stop when I notice the expression on his face.

"I mean it, man. You've got to give her a call.

Don't you dare think about wussing out on me."

"I'll call her."

"You mean it?"

"Yeah, I'll call her. Not tonight, of course. I mean, it's Christmas and she's probably doing family stuff."

JK swishes his wand in the general vicinity of my crotch and chants, "Testicalis enlargus."

I burst into laughter. I'm still laughing as he makes his way into the twilight, his wand at the ready.

December 26

I guess JK's spell worked. I call Charlotte the day after Christmas, and we talk for an hour before I finally get up the nerve to ask her out. She accepts without hesitation. As a fourteen-year-old, a mall date is one of my few options. A movie felt too cliché, although it would have had the advantage of not requiring me to talk, something I wasn't totally sure I could do without coming across as a complete idiot.

I shake my head as I realize Charlotte and I would be what JK call a mall couple. We used to laugh at the mall couples, especially what we call the "slow walkers," those slow-moving pairs walking hand in hand at a pace reserved for giant tortoises, completely oblivious to the fact that other people might want to get around them.

The thought of holding Charlotte's hand as we walk sends me into a panic attack. I can't believe she agreed to go out with me. Butterflies fill my stomach, but it's a good feeling. I try to calm my nerves by replaying in my mind every romantic comedy I have ever seen, trying to remember the smooth lines the guys say that make the girls swoon.

Instead, I keep coming up with things that could go wrong.

December 29

Charlotte opens her door and I am as close to speechless as I have ever been. Despite the bitterly cold temperature, she's wearing a short skirt in a red checkered pattern. Overnight it dipped below zero, and the forecast calls for a high in the single digits, but here she is, with her long legs tanned in the middle of winter.

"Hey, Brian." She smiles, and her dazzling white teeth light up her face, causing my heart to skip a beat. Incapable of words, I nod and grin my own goofy smile back at her.

"Let me grab my coat, okay?" I nod again, wondering if I'm going to regain my ability to speak at some point.

I wait in the cold on the porch, but I no longer notice the temperature or the grayness of the low-hanging clouds. There is a singular point in your life where you discover what love is, and I wonder if this is that moment.

The rest of the day is a blur. We did what I had seen other mall couples do—although it was way too soon for anyone, especially me, to think of us as a couple. We wander aimlessly from store to store, walking and talking. To be fair, she carries the lion's share of the conversation, but I don't care because I'm lost in the song playing quietly under the surface of her words. It's like hearing a symphony for the first time and letting it take hold and carry you away.

We eat lunch at the food court amidst hundreds of people, but I can't see or hear anyone but Charlotte. I can't tell you what we ate or what we talked about, but I can describe in detail how the mall lights reflected off her blue eyes and how her nose crinkled when she laughed.

I remember an interview I saw with a baseball player who was describing how it felt when he hit the cover off the ball. He described it like everything was moving in slow motion. He could see every stitch on the baseball and the direction the ball was rotating. The funny thing, he said, was that he couldn't remember anything else—the crowd, the players, and the field was a blur. It was only him and the baseball.

That's the way this day felt. Everything is a blur but Charlotte, the song her voice makes, her sparkling blue eyes, and her crinkly nose. And those amazing tan legs under her short skirt.

I don't work up the nerve to hold her hand as we walk home, but she does give me a hug on her front porch. The embrace lasts a long time, and yet, it is over in an instant. With a flourish, she's through the door and in the warmth of her house, leaving me alone once again. The temperature is five degrees, with a wind chill below zero, but that hug warms me from my frozen toes to my numb cheeks. If I try, I imagine the clean smell of her shampoo—honeysuckle and lemon—and feel the smoothness of her long brown hair on my cheek. If I try, I feel the touch of her hand on my shoulder as she leans closer. Without trying, I feel the emptiness and coldness of that porch without her presence. I didn't think anything could overcome the wave of euphoria that swept over me that day.

December 30

The week of Christmas détente between my parents ends abruptly with an argument that lasts most of the day. Like a lot of their fights over the past couple of months, it starts over something small.

"Can you grab the butter out of the icebox?" my dad asks as he pulls a couple of slices of toast from the toaster.

I search through the refrigerator, but I don't see the butter container. I'm starting a shelf by shelf search when my dad barks, "What are you doing, churning it? My toast is getting cold."

"I used up the butter last night," my mom says from behind the morning paper.

"Why didn't you say so in the first place?" he

asks and dumps the toast into the trash can.

"Why'd you throw them away?"

"Because I don't like toast without butter."

"Well, someone else might," she says coldly.

"Fine!" He retrieves the two pieces of toast from the trash can. "Here you go!" He tosses them onto the counter, and one of the slices slides off onto the floor, sending crumbs flying under the kitchen table. My mom doesn't say anything as he storms out of the kitchen. She puffs angrily on her cigarette and waves her hand to diffuse the cloud of smoke hanging in front of her face.

Becky reaches over to hold my hand, which is something she's doing more and more lately, as if she's grasping for a life jacket in the middle of a raging sea. To be honest, I appreciate the comfort of her hand as much as she does. As a kid, you feel helpless when your parents fight, too afraid to take sides, too fearful to open your mouth to say the words you want to say.

The argument continues throughout the day. What started with butter makes its way through complaints about the clutter in the living room to my dad drinking too much to my mom overspending at Christmas to finances in general. The fight moves from room to room, topic to topic, with voices raised in anger or lowered in barely controlled rage. Becky and I try to stay out of the fray, but the shifting battle lines make it difficult to avoid it. She is finally able to escape to her friend Casey's house, but I'm not as lucky. JK is down for the count with the flu and Charlotte is out of town, so I am stuck at the center of ground zero.

"Brian, can you bring down the Christmas decoration boxes from the attic?" my mom asks in a terse voice.

"Sure, Mom," I answer, relieved to be doing

something that will take me off the battlefield but crestfallen she's already taking the Christmas decorations down. She usually doesn't start to de-Christmas the house until a week or so after New Year's Day. That we haven't even made it until the end of the year means Christmas will be over and any truce between my parents will be officially declared null and void.

I make my way upstairs and lug my desk chair into the hallway to tug down the rope to the attic. I haven't been up there since the day I saw the snow that hadn't happened yet. With the blur of Christmas and my constant thoughts of Charlotte, I had completely forgotten about the window. The memory comes back with a jolt when I notice how bright the attic is. Light streams out of the rectangle leading up to the room at the top of the stairs. My brain recognizes this doesn't make sense. The heavy clouds that had hung low in the sky as Charlotte and I walked to the mall the previous day are still there, bringing a dull grayness to the day. Lights are on throughout the house even though it is mid-afternoon. And yet, here is a stream of light cascading out of a dark room. A room with a single dusty lightbulb.

The light brings everything in the room to sharp focus. A pile of empty Christmas decoration boxes are stacked haphazardly by the wall where I had left them. I consider picking up a stack of boxes and heading back downstairs, but I'm kidding myself. There's no way I can come up to the attic without taking a look out the window.

I peer through the glass.

No snow.

I'm not fazed by that. After all, I saw snow when there wasn't any, so why should I be surprised to see green grass when the yard should be covered in snow? The grass could use a good mowing, and I make a note to crank up the old lawnmower later today. My gaze shifts. Mr. Crowley has left a giant lawn refuse bag at the end of his driveway. He's got an old lawn mower without a mulching feature, so he bags his grass to be picked up. What's more interesting than his bag of grass is the moving van parked in front of my house. A white paneled truck with the words *Two Men and a Truck* stenciled in large black letters on the side. The engine is running, and a wisp of black exhaust rises from the tailpipe. A muscular guy wearing jeans and a tight-fitting black T-shirt closes the sliding door at the rear of the truck. His right arm is covered in tattoos—skulls and flowers and Chinese characters in different colors are interspersed from his wrist all the way to his shirtsleeve. He finishes securing the rear door and pulls himself into the passenger seat. He takes a swig from a bottle of water, rolls down the window, and then hawks a loogie into the grass in my front yard. As I continue to watch, the truck pulls away from the curb and rolls up the street. Someone wrote *WASH ME* in large, crooked letters in the grime covering the back of the truck.

No longer hidden from view, I spot Mrs. Goldsmith and Mrs. Allen as they talk on the driveway across the street. Mrs. Goldsmith is the neighborhood busybody. If there is something going on in the neighborhood, Mrs. Goldsmith knows about it. "She makes it her business to be in everybody's business" my dad always says. The kids know enough to stay away from her, but adults are drawn to her, like how you can't look away from a car accident you pass on the highway.

Mrs. Allen's gaze follows the moving van as it pulls away, but she's listening attentively to Mrs. Goldsmith, who gestures toward our house. Mrs. Goldsmith takes a pull from her cigarette and resumes talking, enjoying her captive audience. She points one hand down the road in the direction of the departed truck and the other hand in a sweeping motion toward our house again. Smoke from her cigarette follows every arm movement.

At one point I'm sure she glances directly at the window, but there is no indication she sees me.

Two Men and a Truck? Well, I have two questions and a thought. The questions are: what is in the truck, and why was it parked in front of my house?

The thought is that I am starting to lose it. I feel like Jimmy Stewart's character in *It's a Wonderful Life.* George Bailey saw the town sign change from Bedford Falls to Pottersville, and my world is changing before my eyes (literally) and I have no plausible (or even implausible) explanation. If I go downstairs and tell my mom I'm going to mow the lawn, she'll take me to the emergency room for a CAT scan.

Sir, we did a brain scan and we didn't find anything.

That old joke makes me giggle, and I worry when I can't stop.

I'm certainly no expert on the brain, but after what I've begun to call my *snow experience,* I did web searches on the subject of déjà vu. I learned most people have a feeling of already having lived through an experience at some time in their lives, sometimes even a couple of times a year. The people who study the brain think one possible cause might be a small seizure in the areas of the brain used for memory creation and retrieval. The seizures cause a tiny brain glitch—a synapse misfire in the memory region— creating an illusion the event has happened before.

The possibility I might have had a brain seizure doesn't make me feel better.

I did feel better when I learned it wasn't actually déjà vu I was experiencing. Déjà vu is more of a memory, while what I had undergone was precognition—seeing into the future. Scientists don't have much to say about precognition, other than it doesn't exist.

The letter I've been dreading arrives—my first semester grades. I stare at the official-looking envelope for a long time before I work up the nerve to tear it carefully open at the conveniently provided perforations. The first thing that goes through my head upon reading the grades is: *it could be worse.* The second is: *but not by much.*

Name:	*Brian Bingham*
Grade:	*9*
Semester GPA:	*2.33*
Overall GPA:	*2.33*
English Composition	*B*
Biology 1	*C*
Physical Education	*B*
Algebra	*C*
US History	*D*
Keyboarding	*B*

My parents will be okay with the B's. Sure, Becky gets all A's, but she's also eight years old. Who couldn't ace third grade? I can probably explain away the C's in biology and algebra, especially since neither of my parents are particularly strong in math or science, but the D in history is a killer. A grade of D has no excuse. It means I hadn't studied, which isn't quite true since I focused very hard in that class, but not on history. It happens to be the class I share with Charlotte. She sits one row over and two seats in front of me, right between me and Mr. Carlsson. It's bad enough he speaks in a hypnotic monotone, but how can I possibly pay attention to anything he says when I have to look right past Charlotte to see him?

Well, my parents are going to see the grades sooner or later, so I might as well get it over with. I take a deep breath and prepare to meet my fate.

As it turns out, my parents aren't as upset about my grades as I thought they would be. They are arguing—wow, what a shocker—when I drop the envelope on the kitchen table. My mom looks up from the table long enough to glance at my grades, but I don't think she's in the mood to start a war on a second front.

"You're going to need to buckle down next semester, Brian," she says, dropping the report card back down on the table.

"Yes, ma'am," I reply. The less said the better at this point.

My dad doesn't even look at the grades. Discretion being the better part of valor, I take the opportunity to slide out of the kitchen and up the stairs to my room. I look over at the US History book gathering dust on my desk. I consider picking it up and getting started on the material for the upcoming semester, but instead I lay back on my bed and think about Charlotte.

January 4

I've talked to Charlotte a few times on the phone since our date, but I haven't seen her since then. She was friendly enough on the phone, but my limited experience with the opposite sex doesn't give me much to go on. I wish I had JK's confidence. He can walk up to any girl in the school, even the seniors, and strike up a conversation as if they were lifelong friends. He doesn't stumble over his words or look down at his feet. He is, as he describes it, one smooth-talking, bad ass dude. I am...well, whatever the opposite of that is.

Standing at my locker, I spot Charlotte halfway down the hallway. She's storing her coat in her own locker. Her long hair cascades over her red sweater in a pool of shimmering brown. I freeze.

"So, you going to stare at her all day or are you going to make your move?" JK asks.

I hadn't heard him approach.

"I have to get stuff from my locker," I say lamely.

"Going to open it first?" JK teases.

My face warms. I fumble on my first attempt at the combination but manage to get it right the second time. As I open the locker, I steal another quick glance down the hall.

"Don't worry, she's still there. I've got your back." He shakes his head. "Man, if anyone ever needed a wingman, it's you."

I grin. Then I take a deep breath and close my locker firmly.

"You ready?"

"Let's do this," I say, with as much false bravado as I can muster.

I manage to keep a smile on my face, but the walk down the hallway feels like what I imagine it would be to take those last steps between a prison cell and the electric chair. If it wasn't for JK's presence, I probably would have turned into the restroom and waited for the bell before coming out.

"You look like you're about to pass out," JK whispers.

"Bite me," is all I come up with as a response.

"Don't worry, I'll catch you if you fall."

"Thanks."

"But just so you understand, I get the girl if you can't make it all the way there."

"Bite me," I repeat.

We are a couple of lockers away from Charlotte when she turns and sees me. A dazzling white smile comes across her face, and she takes the last few steps to meet me. Before I can stammer out a word, her arms encircle me with a hug. I hug her back cautiously, unsure of the amount of force I should use. I don't want to hold her too tight, but I also don't want her to think I don't want to hug her. Because I most definitely want to hug her.

"What, no hug for me?" JK says with a hurt expression on his face.

Charlotte smiles and gives him a quick hug. I'm relieved it's one of those one-armed, friendly hugs and not the kind of hug she had given me.

The bell rings, signaling it's time for our first class. Charlotte starts to head up the hall, but she stops to turn back in my direction. Seeing her hair twirl over her shoulder as she rotates is like watching a daydream in slow motion. I'm so entranced by this vision of her that I almost miss her words.

"Meet me at lunch?"

I don't respond and look at her as if she's talking to somebody else instead of this tongue-tied fool in the middle of the hallway. My reverie is broken by JK's sharp elbow into my ribs.

"The answer is yes, dumbass," he whispers, although loud enough for Charlotte to hear.

"Yes, dumbass," I quip with nervous laughter.

Charlotte smiles her dazzling smile and turns again. My gaze, as well as that of most of the other freshmen guys in the hallway, follow her down the hall.

"Did you just call her a dumbass?" JK asks. He bursts into laughter.

THE WINDOW

That night I try to keep to my promise to buckle down. Charlotte is in a different history class this semester, so at least I don't have that distraction anymore. That doesn't make the material—the economic impact of inventions in the eighteenth century—or Mr. Carlsson's monotonous voice any more interesting. I'm two chapters behind in reading with our first test coming up in a couple of weeks. I manage to make it through one chapter, but it's dry stuff, and I'm not sure how much I will remember. I think back to JK's Christmas present and joking that I hoped it was the answer key to the history test. Although I love where things are going with Charlotte, the answer key is looking pretty good right now.

January 7

It's my second official date with Charlotte. I spend more than an hour picking out what to wear, settling on jeans, a pullover sweater, and my favorite sneakers. Under advisement from JK, I'm taking her to see a movie at the cineplex. To be honest, taking guidance from JK is a risky proposition. Not that he means any harm, but sometimes his recommendations are perfect for a smooth-talking, bad ass dude and not so perfect for a meek, tongue-tied guy like me.

"Seriously, man, it's got to be a horror movie," he informs me.

"I'm not taking her to a slasher flick."

"No, I'm talking about something with a haunted house or occult thing."

"Why, so she can snuggle up to me for protection?"

"Exactly! And here's the deal. There's actually a scientific basis for the whole thing."

"This I've got to hear," I say.

"Horror movies produce an adrenaline rush. It literally gets a girl's heart racing. As far as a physical reaction, it's the closest feeling to love there is."

I laugh, but I then see the seriousness on JK's face. He means it.

So, here I am, sitting in the seven-thirty showing of *House of Fear*, with a tub of popcorn between Charlotte and me. Thinking ahead, I went for the unbuttered popcorn, not wanting to have butter all over my hands on the off chance I might get the opportunity to hold her hand at some point in the evening. No luck so far, but our fingers did touch briefly as we reached into the tub. For me, it was like an electric shock. I jerked my hand out, spilling popcorn all over our laps. Charlotte giggled, but embarrassment heated my face. Luckily, with the lights dimmed and the previews running, I don't think she noticed. I can still feel the touch of her fingers on mine.

The previews end, and the movie begins. The plot is ridiculous and doesn't get better as the film proceeds. A pair of teenagers are spending the night in a haunted house on a dare from their friends. The idea was for the friends to scare the couple, but one by one the friends vanish, each disappearance eliciting shrieks from the audience. Charlotte edges closer and closer, until I can no longer focus on the movie. All I know is the closeness of her and the feel of her arm against mine. I want to put my arm around her—JK would have done it within the first five minutes of the lights dimming—but I can't summon the courage to make my move.

Now the friends have all disappeared and the house, or an entity in the house, is after the couple. Tension is high, and Charlotte has drawn even closer to me, wrapping her arms around mine and resting her head on my shoulder.

I'll never doubt JK's advice again.

I'm afraid to move, not wanting to take the slightest chance I might spoil this moment. Then the next thing I know, the movie and the moment are over.

Charlotte releases my arm and breathes a sigh of relief. "That was a lot scarier than I thought it would be."

"Yeah," I answer, hoping she doesn't ask me anything about the movie because I have absolutely no idea how it ended.

We hold hands on the way back to her house, and I give myself props for going with the unbuttered popcorn. She lingers on the porch, maybe waiting to see if I will kiss her. For me, the snuggle during the movie and holding her hand on the way back are all I can take for one evening. After small talk about enjoying the date, she unlocks the door, smiles her dazzling smile, and enters the house.

I walk home ten feet off the ground, while feeling the warmth of her hand in mine.

JK would have kissed her, but then he is one smooth-talking, bad ass dude. He's a sprinter and I'm a guy learning to walk. Still, I didn't have complaints about how the evening had gone.

January 8

A day after my date with Charlotte, I'm back at the movie theater with my sister Becky. This is a bit unusual for me, as we don't have much of a relationship as far as brothers and sisters go. The age difference has a lot to do with it. My parents separated for eighteen months when I was four years old. I don't have much recollection of the separation, just vague memories of sleeping in a pup tent in the spare room in my dad's apartment on the nights I stayed with him. Then they got back together, my dad moved back in, and a few years later Becky was born. It wasn't long before I had grown tired of all the attention she got. She grows more tolerable as she gets older, but the age difference doesn't shrink.

The movie isn't bad. One good thing about having a younger sister is I get to watch all the animated movies without being ridiculed by my friends. "Yeah, I had to take my little sister to see Toy Story 4 this weekend," I would say, and laugh as everyone rolled their eyes. Truth be told, I had teared up during the conclusion to the movie, but none of my friends—not even JK—would hear that part of the story.

We grab lunch at the food court in the mall—a large chicken sub and fries for me and a kid's chicken nugget meal for Becky. Afterward, we walk home and laugh about our favorite parts of the movie on the way. All in all, it's a pretty good afternoon.

When we get to our driveway, I look up at our house. The roof is covered in snow, although the few remaining icicles are dripping in the warmth of the afternoon sun. If the weather stays like this, the snow will be gone in a couple of days. Looking up, I search the front of the house for the octagonal attic window, but I don't see it.

Thinking my angle is wrong, I walk through the softening snow until I'm in the center of the yard, standing on the remains of the snow fort JK and I had built weeks earlier. I scan the front of the house, but all I see is the dark green siding.

"What are you looking at?" Becky asks.

"Nothing."

"Well, you have to be looking at something."

"It's nothing." And truer words were never spoken. There is no attic window to be found.

"Well, I'm going in the house. I'm freezing," Becky flips her ponytail as she walks up the driveway.

I take one more glance at the house before following my sister inside. I kick off my soggy tennis shoes in the mudroom and head upstairs to the attic. The attic is well-lit with sunlight streaming through the window. I look out the window and see the footprints where I had stood minutes earlier. *If I can see my footprints, then why couldn't I see the window from the yard?*

"Curiouser and curiouser," I say, quite appropriately, as I was beginning to feel like I had followed Alice down a rabbit hole.

I pick at my dinner that night. My silence goes unnoticed as Becky chatters nonstop about the movie and lunch and her new classmate and the upcoming science fair and a number of other topics interesting to third graders. My mom pretends to listen, nodding occasionally, but my dad hides behind the sports page. Pitchers and catchers will report to spring training in less than a month, so every baseball pundit is making early predictions for the season.

I'm a big baseball fan, especially when the team is playing well, but my thoughts are on the window in the attic.

January 18

Another grueling history class ends as the bell rings. The lesson mostly went in one ear and out the other.

"Remember to read up through chapter 28," Mr. Carlsson says as we gather papers and pencils and cram them into backpacks for our next class. "And yes, it will be on the next test."

A collective groan follows the exiting students into the hallway.

I walk out of the classroom, head down in dejected silence.

"Just keep repeating, it's only a test, it's only a test, it's only a test," JK says as he walks up beside me.

"Easy for you to say," I snap, immediately regretting my tone. "I mean, you got this stuff down. If I fail this test, my parents are going to kill me."

"Probably," he says thoughtfully. "If they do, can I have your bedroom?" He asks this with such earnestness I'm forced to laugh. He punches me in one arm and grins. "They're not going to kill you, buddy, and you want to know why?"

"Why?" I ask, hoping he has a solution for me.

"Because you're going to go home tonight and open up that book and learn this stuff. Or else."

"Or else what?"

"Or else I'll have your room *and* your girlfriend." He smiles a devilish grin and dashes off before I can respond.

The thought of losing Charlotte to my best friend is a sobering thought. It is enough to get me to study that night. I don't catch up on all the reading, but I do manage to get through a couple of chapters. Even though the material is as dry as dust, I keep at it. I'm feeling pretty good about my accomplishment when I reach the end of the section. With growing confidence, I take the section review test, circling the answers to the multiple-choice questions. Even though the chapter is fresh on my mind, when I check the answer key, I managed to get about half of the questions right.

I toss the book onto the floor in frustration. Looking around the room, I wonder how JK is going to like his new digs.

January 22

On my way to the bathroom before bed, I pass under the doorway to the attic. As always, I look up at what is becoming a distraction only surpassed by Charlotte and notice the door isn't quite flush with the ceiling. A small crack of light runs the length of the opening. My impulse is to ignore it. My history test is fast approaching, and I need to read another chapter before turning in for the night. My parents aren't going to look past another D, and I picture a lonely summer with me stuck grounded in my room. Worse, with me out of action, I picture Charlotte dating a number of guys over the summer. I've seen other guys in school giving her the eye, and I cringe every time. With my mission clear, I ignore the hatchway and return to my room with the intention of devoting the next hour to the study of the telegraph, the steamboat, the gas turbine, and, of course, Eli Whitney and his damn cotton gin.

My rational mind knows the winter sun had set hours earlier, so there's no way that crack of light can exist, but I need to see it for myself. Fifteen minutes later, I find myself in the attic. Perched on a seat in front of the window at nine o'clock at night, I look out on my brightly lit front yard. Mr. Horrigan, who lives in the house at the corner, walks by with Knute, his little wiener dog. Mr. Horrigan's face is wrapped in a giant green scarf, and Knute's ridiculously long body is clad in a bright green sweater with **Go Irish** in bright yellow script.

Other than Mr. Horrigan and his dog, there isn't much else to see outside. Based on Mr. Horrigan's attire, it's bitterly cold, and the streets are clear except for an occasional car. Still, I continue to watch, as though the window has called out to me and there is something it wants me to see.

Great, now I think the window is talking to me. I am losing it.

I watch for an hour or more, all thoughts of Eli Whitney driven from my mind, but there isn't much to see. A UPS truck drives by, pausing momentarily in front of the Goldsmith's house before it continues down the street. Even though the scene doesn't change, I continue my vigil, taking in every detail of my limited view. And that's when I spot it.

I don't think I would have noticed it at all if not for the wind blowing across the front of the house, a gust stiff enough to flutter the front page of the small stack of papers. The papers—four or five pages stapled together—are flapping in the breeze at the edge of the roofline. One corner, the one containing the silver staple, dips into the gutter. I lean closer. My forehead touches the frosty glass.

The title on the front page: **American History Test – Eighteenth Century Inventions**. I draw back quickly from the window, nearly toppling over in my chair in my haste to put distance between me and the glass. I close my eyes, but I continue to see the brightness of the sunlight streaming through the window. I take a deep breath, open my eyes, and look out the window again. The papers are still there, fluttering in the breeze.

I try to think it through reasonably, but what about a one-way window that allows me to see into the future is reasonable? The window had been right about the Christmas snow, right down to the slightest detail. And the stack of papers resembles the tests

Mr. Carlsson gives, so there is no reason to think they aren't legit. The prospect that *the* test—the one I was going to take in ten days—is sitting outside this window is too much to resist.

That leads to other questions: Does the window even open? Is it possible to reach into the future? And will the window let me bring something back from the other side?

The question I don't consider is whether there will be consequences to my next actions.

I've never noticed the hinges on the octagonal window or the tiny latch. The thought the window might open has never crossed my mind. But there it is, right in front of me. One small latch keeping me from reaching out and grabbing the stack of papers. The test, if that's what it really is, slides several inches farther down the shingled roof and flutters in the gutter. Another gust of wind may take the test over the edge and into the bushes below. Or maybe the test will disappear when it leaves the limited view the window affords me.

The idea of losing the test seals my decision. Without another thought, I lift the latch and push the window open in one fluid motion. A blast of frigid air floods the attic. The wind has strengthened, and the pages teeter on the edge of the roof. Firmly grasping one edge of the window for support, I stretch my hand toward the papers—and freeze. Not from the cold air cascading over my arm but from the appearance of my arm, which appears transparent as it shimmers in a golden light. I can see the shingles through my arm. I'm horrified by the sight but transfixed by what I'm seeing. One moment my arm is solid, and I can see the hairs on my pale skin rising in response to the cold. A fraction of a second later, my arm is no longer there, and the cold is replaced by a feeling of soothing warmth, as if my arm is being engulfed in a blanket of incredible softness.

I stare as my arm fades in and out of existence, unable to move or look away. Through my arm—in one of those moments when it no longer appears—I see the stack of papers shift as the wind threatens to pull them out of the gutter and out of my reach. Without thinking, I stretch farther, watching as first my elbow and then my shoulder disappear as they clear the window frame. Then my arm and shoulder fade back into view, and my fingers brush the edge of the papers. I pinch the stack between fingers as they blink in and out of view and pull the test back through the window.

I close the window firmly, taking care to make sure the latch is refastened. As I do, the window goes black for a moment as daylight transitions into night. Then light appears again, not the bright light of a sunlit day but the dull glow of the streetlights and the single bulb over the Goldsmith's front door. The attic goes dark. I sway for a moment as a wave of dizziness passes over me, and I fall heavily into the chair. I close my eyes and put my head between my knees until I no longer feel the urge to throw up.

Then I look down at my hand. The test is grasped between my thumb and middle finger.

I lay in bed, rereading the test for what must be the tenth time as my mind races. I turn out the lights and stare into the darkness. I try to turn off my thoughts, too, but it's impossible. Sleep doesn't come for a long time as I think about Pastor Mark's sermons on God.

My parents make sure to get Becky and me to church most Sundays, although their own attendance has become more and more spotty over the years. Now that I'm older, I've been going to the church service instead of Sunday school. The sermons sound like a dichotomy of two entirely different Gods. There is the all-loving God of the New Testament, the one who gives me hope for forgiveness. Tonight, though, my thoughts are on the Old Testament God, the one who isn't going to let me get away with anything. Fire, brimstone, and a life in Hell awaits me because of that chocolate bar I snitched from the grocery store two summers ago. The Old Testament God is always asking for a bloody sacrifice to be placed on his altar. I wonder if there will be a sacrifice required for pulling this test through the window.

February 1

Let's face it. I'm cheating on this test, so I'm terrified on two fronts. One, that I'll get caught. What's left of my rational mind tells me there's no way for anyone to find out I have a copy of the test, but there's not much that's normal in my world these days. Still, getting caught is the lesser of my two concerns. The thing I am more worried about is that the test sitting face down on my desk bears absolutely no resemblance to the one I used for my study guide. I've heard one of the most common bad dreams people have is about showing up in class for a test you haven't studied for, and there is a good chance that is exactly what is about to happen. I don't have a backup plan. I studied hard, but only for the questions on the five sheets of paper I pulled through the window ten nights ago.

"Okay, you can turn your test over and begin." I look up and Mr. Carlsson is staring directly at me.

I haven't even turned the test over, and he is on to me.

The moment of truth has arrived. Around the room my classmates turn their papers over, and pencils begin to scratch as they start working on their tests. I look at the back of the test, transfixed by the silver staple clamping the pages together in one corner.

I take a deep breath and turn the test over.

I smile.

It is the same test sitting securely in the top drawer of my desk at home. Every page is identical. I sigh to calm myself, and then I set to work on the test. I answer each question, spend twenty minutes scribbling my well-rehearsed answer to the essay question, and even use a few minutes to double-check my answers. When I look at the clock, I'm shocked to see there are twenty minutes of class time remaining. I couldn't turn in my test too early or it would look suspicious, so I trace over each of my answers to make it appear as though I am still working. I'm scared of getting caught, but I can't help smiling to myself.

I wait for JK and a few of my other classmates to lay their tests on Mr. Carlsson's desk before I rise from my seat and place mine on top of the stack. I can feel my teacher's gaze boring into the back of my head as I walk toward the door. I wait for him to call me back, but I make it safely out of the classroom.

JK is joking with a couple of junior girls when I enter the hallway. "Catch you later, ladies," he says, giving an exaggerated bow as he backs away from the group. Brittany Morgan giggles and blushes. Was there something there JK hasn't told me about? I thought he was in between girlfriends, but those in-between periods never lasted longer than a week or two.

"You look like you survived, at least," he says as I approach. "In fact, you look pretty darn cheerful for coming out of one of Mr. Carlsson's tests." He eyes me suspiciously.

"Wasn't too bad." I shrug. "I guess I managed to study the right stuff this time."

The right stuff? The exact *stuff is more like it.*

JK gives me a long look.

"So, what's the deal with Brittany?" I ask in what I hope isn't an obvious attempt to change the subject.

JK isn't buying it. "Nothing to tell. The women all love me. Now, about this test—"

I'm saved by the bell indicating it's time for our next class.

"Gotta run, man," I say. "Algebra class. Catch you after school."

February 3

The history test makes me a believer. Mr. Carlsson lays it on my desk and pauses to take a long look at me. I glance down and see 98% at the top of the first page.

"Nice work, Brian. Highest grade in the class," he says, while searching my face for some sign.

A sign of what? That I cheated on the test? Will he believe me if I confess to reaching into the future and pulling the questions out of thin air?

"Thank you, Mr. Carlsson," I reply. My voice is steady although my heart races.

He continues to hand out tests as he walks down the aisle, occasionally commenting to a classmate. I take this time to look through the test, trying to figure out where I had missed those two points. There it is. He took the points off my answer to the essay question: What impact did the invention of the cotton gin have on the growth of slavery? I could probably argue my case for those final two points. After all, I had Googled the question and studied the rationale presented by a Harvard economics professor on this topic. I suspect his answer was better than anything Mr. Carlsson could come up with. Instead, I turn back to the front page and smile at the 98% circled in red.

JK cranes his neck from the next row and sees my score.

"What the hell, man? I thought you were failing

this class."

"Not anymore," I respond and look down at my score again. "Not anymore."

"Maybe you can give me pointers," he says, looking down at the 81% on his own test.

"Yeah, sure."

* * *

My dad is surprised to see my test score when I drop it on the coffee table. He pushes aside the ash tray overflowing with crushed butts and pulls the test in front of him.

"A ninety-eight, huh? What happened to the other two points?"

I can't tell if he's joking at first. My dad has a biting humor, which is usually funny but sometimes crosses over into meanness.

"I must have dropped them on the way home from school," I respond, hoping he's in the mood for funny instead of mean.

"Nice job, kid." He smiles.

I'm relieved to see that smile. It's a rare occurrence these days.

"Nothing to it."

Yeah, nothing to it if you know the test questions a week in advance.

"Isn't this the class you've been struggling with?"

"Yeah, but I studied pretty hard for this test."

"Good to see." He lights another cigarette, exhales a plume of smoke, and returns his attention to the evening news on the television.

Lying in the dark in my bed that night, I wonder what it means. The test made it real, but what was "real" anymore?

7

February 4

After a restless night, I climb groggily out of bed. On the way to the bathroom, I look down at my desk. My test is sitting on top of a stack of papers, with 98% circled in red.

I couldn't have done it without seeing the questions ahead of time, could I?

Besides, I have the proof. I pull open the top drawer.

It's empty.

Twenty minutes later, Becky pokes her head into my room "What are you doing?"

I look up in in frustration. I've torn my desk completely apart. Every drawer is out, and I upended my trashcan. Gum wrappers, a broken pencil, and crumpled scraps of paper sit in a pile in the middle of my room. My bookbag is turned inside out, and I examined and reexamined every piece of paper. The blank test is nowhere to be found.

"I'm cleaning my room."

"You have a strange way of doing it," she replies. With a shrug, she disappears from the doorway, and her bare feet pad down the stairs.

I lay back on the floor, staring at the ceiling, unsure of what to do next.

The window is real. If the snow isn't evidence enough, the history test sure as hell proves it, and there's no going back now. People say what you don't know can't hurt you, but I don't think that's true. The future is going to come whether I know about it or not.

THE WINDOW

Ten minutes later, I'm back in front of the window. The more time I spend in the attic, the more confused I get. Most days, the window is a plain window and I'm limited to what I can see out of it. To one side is Mr. Crowley's driveway, partially blocked by the large elm tree in our front yard. On the other side I see the Allen's driveway and part of their trimmed yard. Across the street, I see most of the Goldsmith's house and about half of Adam Pollock's house. Adam is two years older than Becky, who is way too young to be thinking about boys, by the way, but she giggles more than usual whenever he is around.

I feel a sense of relief when the window is nothing more than a pane of glass. On those days, it's a viewport into a mundane world where kids play in the yard and cars go by and the future is a mystery. For a moment, I wonder if people outside will begin to think of me as the crazy boy in the attic if they look up and see me. I smile at this thought until I remember you can't see this window from outside the house.

But I'm sure Mrs. Goldsmith had looked right at me when the moving van pulled away. Had she seen me or the faded green vinyl siding spanning the front of our house?

Other days the window is—what?

An illusion? A portal into the future? A tiny seizure in my brain?

Maybe there will be enough seizures that my brain will seize up entirely one day. I picture my parents finding me lifeless on the attic floor in front of a dusty section of drywall with no clue as to what had happened or why I had been in the attic in the first place.

On those days, when the window is more than a piece of glass separating me from the outside world, time barely moves, like a film in slow-motion, allowing me to see everything in stark detail.

48

And then there were days like today, when the window doesn't show anything but a swirling mix of gray. The fog reminds me of a trip to California when I was Becky's age. My mom and I had tagged along on my dad's business meeting in San Francisco. While he discussed topics like variable expenses, annuity tables, and return on investment, my mom and I explored the city. On our last day, we took a taxi to Twin Peaks, where the brochures promised a "spectacular 360-degree view of San Francisco," with "amazing views of the Pacific Ocean, the Golden Gate Bridge, Alcatraz, and downtown skyscrapers." Instead, we saw nothing but a gray blanket of fog. No ocean, no buildings, no Berkeley and Oakland across the bay, no Mount Diablo in the distance. Nothing but chilly, churning fog in all directions. We had waited in the damp cold for more than an hour, hoping for the fog to clear, before giving up and taking another cab back to our hotel.

While the San Francisco fog had been cold, there's something about the undulating gray outside the window that's inviting, as if it would welcome me as a friend into a warm embrace. I stare at the swirling gray for hours and picture myself disappearing into its midst as it carries me away.

February 11

I've avoided going into the attic for the past week, although I have an Algebra test coming up and wonder if those questions might be tucked under a loose shingle outside the window. I have other things on my mind today, though. My first Valentine's with Charlotte is approaching, and I'm trying to figure out something romantic for us to do.

The doorbell rings, interrupting my thoughts of a candlelit dinner while Charlotte gazes into my eyes.

"Brian!" Becky yells up the stairs. "JK is here."

"Send him up," I holler back.

JK's size eleven feet pound up the stairs, and he bursts into my room. He tosses his coat on my bed and plops into the worn beanbag chair in the corner. A whoosh of air and a few loose beans fly out of a small tear in one side. I make a mental note to slap another piece of duct tape over the rip.

"What's up, man?" I ask.

"Valentine's Day. Got it figured out yet?"

I start to explain my tentative plans, but JK peers at me sadly and shakes his head. "Wrong."

"What's wrong with a nice dinner?"

"Two things. First, everybody is doing dinner that night, which means long waits and a waiter standing over you, giving you the stink eye to get you to finish up. His tip's not getting bigger while you sit there taking up space. Plus, there's a table between the two of you. What's romantic about that?"

"I guess you're right, but—"

"And second," JK continues, "I have a better plan."

I groan in protest, but I'm secretly anxious to hear what he has to say. He has a lot more experience in the area of dating, and he's been right on every step with Charlotte, from the note to the horror movie, so he may know what he's talking about. Clearly, I don't.

"Well, spill it."

"Ice skating."

"Seriously, ice skating?"

"Serious as a heart attack, and, like all of my brilliant ideas, there's science behind this one, too."

"Okay, let's hear it." I toss his coat on the floor and belly-flop onto my bed.

"Here goes. First, eighty-two percent of couples hold hands when they skate. That means you'll be in constant contact with her the whole night. Second, it's cold, so she'll want to snuggle up with you. More than sixty-five percent of couples report more snuggling during ice skating than other activities. And finally, forty-three percent of all couples had their first kiss after ice skating."

He sits back with a satisfied look on his face.

"And one hundred percent of those statistics were pulled right out of your ass, weren't they?"

"Give or take a percent or two, yes." He grins.

"And how do you know we haven't already had our first kiss?"

JK stares at me. A smile plays across his lips. "Are you telling me you could have kept that secret from me?"

My friend knows me too well. I would have shouted it from the rooftops. It might have even made the evening news.

"Seriously, though," he says, "why don't you guys come with Brittany and me?"

So, he did have something with Brittany! At least I had called that one right.

"But what if she can't skate?"

"Then she'll have to hold onto you for balance."

"And what if she's a much better skater than me?"

"Then you'll have to hold onto her for balance." JK gives a sly wink.

"You thought this one out, didn't you?"

"It's what I do. Hey, does your mom have any of those delicious chocolate chip cookies she always makes for me?"

I raise a brow. "For you?"

"Well, I am her favorite son, you know."

February 14

Valentine's Day doesn't disappoint when it comes to the weather. There's been talk of a warm front coming through the area, but the temperature is in the mid-twenties with a slight breeze. Charlotte wears a short black skirt, her red tights that match her bright red lipstick, and her hair is pulled back with something she calls a scrunchie. The name is stupid, but she looks amazing with a ponytail.

It's cold enough to keep a lot of people away from the outdoor rink, so the four of us have plenty of room to skate. Pop music blares from the speakers, and everyone is in a festive mood. Charlotte turns out to be a good ice skater but insists on holding hands. There are no objections from me. During the slower songs, Charlotte cuddles closer as we skate.

JK and Brittany cruise by us during a romantic song, and JK nods and mouths "told you so" as they pass.

I smile and nod back.

While the Zamboni driver is smoothing out the ice, the four of us buy s'more kits from the concession stand and roast the marshmallows over one of the fire pits.

Charlotte snuggles under my arm for warmth.

"Sixty-five percent," JK says. "Although the number may be going up tonight."

Charlotte and Brittany look confused, but I laugh.

"Inside joke," I whisper to Charlotte when she asks what it means. "I'll tell you later."

I stuff the gooey marshmallow between the chocolate bar and graham cracker and squeeze, so the white fluff spills out on all four sides.

"Perfect," Charlotte says as I hand her the sticky mess. She takes a large bite and purrs with delight.

It's Valentine's Day. It's dark. It's romantic in front of a cozy fire. It's the perfect time to move in for that first kiss.

And I freeze.

Even though everything is telling me this is the

moment, I can't do it. Instead, I reach for another marshmallow and spend the next thirty seconds arranging it on the sharpened stick. I steal a glance over at JK, but he and Brittany are locked together in a long kiss. I blew my opportunity, so I glumly hold the marshmallow over the fire and turn it to roast it on all sides.

The night has turned colder, and Charlotte nestles under my arm as the four of us walk home, laughing at JK's continuous stream of jokes. We reach the corner where we will part ways, and JK nods to Brittany. They come to an abrupt stop.

"Okay, dude, this is where it happens," JK says.

"Where what happens?"

"First kiss, man. Let's do this."

"You and me?" I ask, nervously trying to deflect the conversation.

"Now or never, buddy."

I glance over at Charlotte. She gazes into my eyes and leans in a couple of inches. I lean in the other four, and our lips touch. I taste marshmallow and chocolate, and then the moment carries me away. It's one of the shortest kisses in the history of first kisses, but I don't care. I kissed her!

Not knowing what to do next, I blurt out "Ta da!" And then I feel my cheeks burning in embarrassment as everyone laughs.

"Seriously? Ta da?" JK says.

Brittany giggles.

Charlotte comes to my defense "It was worth a ta da." And that is the moment I'm sure I love her.

Their mission accomplished, JK and Brittany turn and, hand in hand, walk down the street. JK turns one more time to yell, "Forty-two percent, bro!"

"I thought it was forty-three," I yell back.

JK's laughter rings in the air as Charlotte and I kiss a second time, without the pressure of an audience. I'm already getting better at it.

8

March 3

I'm happy to be headed over to JK's house for a couple of hours of guy time. I haven't seen him since Valentine's Day, because I've been busy with Charlotte and he's been spending more time with Brittany. My parents are in the middle of another argument—this one started over a newspaper editorial—and I make the wise decision not to interrupt by asking for a ride. The Wilson's house is a couple of blocks away, so I slosh through the melting snow.

JK meets me at the door and stares at my soaked sneakers.

"Drop 'em on the mat, dude," he says. "Mrs. Wilson already mopped twice today."

I take off my shoes and set them on the welcome mat next to two pairs of JK's muddy sneakers.

"How are things going with Brittany?" I ask when we settle onto the couch in the basement, waiting for his old Xbox to boot up.

"Okay, I guess."

"Not exactly a five-star review there."

JK shrugs. "She's okay, but she's high maintenance, you know?"

I laugh. JK's ideal girlfriend is someone who fawns over him, which is usually the case. I wonder if Brittany is high maintenance or if she's making JK work harder on the relationship than he's used to having to do.

"And how are things going with my girl Charlotte?" JK asks.

"Your girl?"

"Well, she would be if I wanted to rescue her from that troll she's so enamored with. All it would take is one long look in my dark brown eyes."

That comment leads to a vigorous wrestling match. JK has me by about four inches and twenty pounds, so it doesn't take him long to pin me against the couch cushion. He's preparing to shove an embroidered pillow into my face when Mrs. Wilson yells down the stairs.

"Are you boys roughhousing?"

We roll our eyes.

"No, ma'am," JK calls back.

I stifle a giggle.

"Okay, because I don't want to have to buy a new couch because you boys broke it."

"We're playing on the Xbox," JK responds. "The couch is good. I promise."

The door at the top of the stairs closes, and we break into laughter.

"You're lucky she saved you," JK says, "because I was about to kick your butt."

He tosses me a controller, and we start a game of Madden Football. It's a few years old—not the latest edition I have at my house—but he beats me anyway. That's the thing with JK. He doesn't make a big deal about what he doesn't have and makes the best of what he does have. He picks up most of his clothes at the thrift shop but manages to be the most stylish guy at school. My mom buys me the latest stuff and I look like a slob next to JK. Something inside him shines through.

As I put on my shoes in preparation for the wet slosh home, I want to tell JK it was great hanging with him, but guys don't do that, so I wave a hand, toss out a casual insult, and trudge home through the slush.

March 10

A storm spits freezing rain at the attic window. Rivulets of water move down the glass and freeze as they reach the casement at the bottom. I've been sitting in front of the window for more than an hour. I should be studying, but instead I'm staring out at nothing. My thoughts are as clear as the freezing water. The wind picks up, driving the water sideways across the window.

A wet glob of papers plasters itself against the window. I jump back in alarm, and then watch as the papers slide down the glass and onto the slope of the roof.

I leap to my feet. Opening the window, I'm assaulted with a spray of freezing rain and wind. Ignoring the sudden cold, I reach out blindly, feeling for the stack of papers on the roof. My fingers brush over a page, and I grab the bundle. Before I can get them safely into the attic, though, a furious burst of wind rips three or four pages from my hand and flings them off the roof. I pull in the rest and quickly close the window.

It's the Algebra mid-term, or the first five pages of it, anyway. I spend the next half hour drying the pages with my mom's blow dryer. There are a couple of blurred questions due to the thorough soaking the pages received, but it's enough. I spend the rest of the evening working out solutions to the problems.

March 19

I ring Charlotte's doorbell and wait for her to answer. We're heading out to dinner at the Pizza Chef down the street and then going to play indoor miniature golf. It's not fancy, it's not romantic, but it's perfect. After two months of dating, I'm finally feeling comfortable with Charlotte, as though we really should be going out. There's a lot of self-doubt, which may never go away, but I no longer feel as if I'm masquerading when I'm with her.

She answers the door and smiles, and I breathe a sigh of relief it's not her dad's stern face staring out at me. The weather has warmed up over the week, and the snow is finally gone. I don't think winter is over yet, but there are signs spring might not be too far away.

"Bye, Mom," she yells into the house before closing the front door and taking my hand. Her hand feels small and warm in mine. A slight tingle runs up my arm. I can't help but give her one of my lopsided smiles. We exchange comfortable small talk on the way to the restaurant about school and homework and mutual friends—not too many of these since Charlotte runs in a much more elite crowd than I could ever hope to join.

After dinner, she picks up the bill.

"You don't have to do that," I protest.

"Nope, it's my turn." She takes cash from her purse as if the matter is settled.

My mild protestations aside, I'm relieved because I've been going through a lot of cash. My lawn mowing income won't start again for another couple of months, and I hate asking my parents for money, especially since the subject of finances is a bitter topic at our house.

The miniature golf course is a short walk away. While Charlotte picks out a putter, I pay for the round.

"What color balls?"

"Huh?" The question interrupts me staring at Charlotte.

The older guy working the counter, with long greasy hair and a scraggly beard, takes a long look in her direction and nods appreciatively. "What color balls you want?"

"Yellow, I guess. And purple for my girlfriend." I make a point to emphasize *girlfriend.*

"I figured you more for a blue ball kind of guy," the greasy-haired guy says. He snickers.

I ignore the comment and meet Charlotte at the first hole. When I hand her the golf ball, she smiles. "Purple is my favorite color."

I knew that, if her usual choice of scrunchie color was an indication.

She may have been trying to mess up my aim, but Charlotte waits until I'm lining up a putt on the third hole when she asks, "So how come you've never introduced me to your family?"

Because I didn't figure you'd go out with me more than a couple of times went immediately through my mind, but I don't want her to know that.

"I guess because your house is on the way to everything we do," I say.

"Really?" She raises an eyebrow. "That's your story?"

"It's my story, and I'm sticking with it." I grin, hoping it will end the subject.

It doesn't.

"Do they even know you're going out with someone?"

"Of course."

Well, they're vaguely aware I've been spending time with someone other than JK.

"Hmm."

I look up from my putter and see a frown on her face.

"Hey, my sister is having a birthday party in a couple of weeks. Why don't you come over and meet everyone then?"

"It's a date." She smiles, and the twinkle returns to her beautiful blue eyes.

Relieved, I line up my putt. The ball flies past the

hole and bounces over the wooden border and onto the concrete walkway.

She laughs. "Maybe golf isn't your game."

April 8

I am nervous about Charlotte meeting my parents. I'm sure they'll love her—how could they not—but I worry about how she is going to like them.

"Brian, can you check in the pantry to see if we have napkins?" my mom asks.

"I thought you bought napkins," my dad says. "They were on the list."

"I guess I forgot."

"Why can't you check things off the list like a normal person?"

And the war is on.

I secretly side with my dad on this one. What's the point of making a list if you don't check to make sure you bought everything on the list? Still, it isn't worth starting World War III because a bunch of eight-year-olds might get chocolate icing on their party dresses. I escape the fighting—temporarily, at least—by volunteering to ride my bike to the store to pick up napkins and anything else my mom may have forgotten.

I'm worried because I want the party to go well. To be honest, it isn't so much for Becky's sake as for mine. This is the first family event I'm bringing Charlotte to, and I want her to like my family as much as I do. That's impossible, of course, but for the simple survival of our sanity, we can look past our own family's faults and pick out those imperfections elsewhere. Charlotte's mom, for example, makes this horrible snorting sound when she laughs. Charlotte's younger brother Charlie insists on following us around the house whenever I'm over there. He's never more than five feet away, which seriously cuts into any kissing action. I suspect Charlotte's dad has Charlie spying on us. Her dad doesn't like me much. He's civil enough, I guess—he insists on shaking my hand when he answers the door—but there is a cold detachment that is discomforting. I talked to my dad about it, and he provided a blunt explanation.

"It's simple, Brian," he said. "You aren't good enough for his daughter."

I stared at him in shock and total dejection.

My dad laughed at my reaction. "It's not you, Son. No one is good enough for his daughter. You could walk on water and shit gold bricks and you'd never be good enough. And I'll let you in on a secret. No guy will be good enough for your sister, either. It has nothing to do with you. It's something about fathers and daughters."

"What about sons? Is anyone good enough for them?"

My dad laughs. "It's different with sons. The goal with boys is to make sure they're not living in our basement ten years after college."

The explanation makes me feel better but knowing Charlotte's dad will never like me isn't going to make our future encounters easier.

When I get back from the store, my dad is smoking out on the front porch and my mom is crying in the kitchen. I drop the plastic sack containing the napkins and a package of plastic forks on the counter and stand a few feet from my mom. She dabs her eyes with a tissue and gives me a quick hug.

"Thanks, Brian," she says through a brave smile. "I'd forget my head if it wasn't attached."

"We all forget things, Mom."

"Tell that to your father." It's a snarky comment,

and I can tell she regrets it immediately. That is one thing with my parents. They fight a lot, but they do a pretty good job of keeping Becky and me out of the fray. I can't remember either of my parents saying something negative about the other in front of us. My mom's snide remark is about as bad as it ever gets. Not that this makes the constant bickering any easier to deal with.

Charlotte arrives about an hour before the party. She's dressed casually, but jeans and a sweatshirt have never looked so good. I take in a long look at her as she shivers on the front porch.

"Aren't you going to ask her in?" my mom asks, wiping her hands on a dish cloth as she comes up behind me.

"Um, yeah. Come in."

I step aside and hold the door as Charlotte enters. She shakes my mom's hand and shows off her dazzling smile.

"It's nice to meet you, Mrs. Bingham."

"Thank you, Charlotte. It's nice to *finally* meet you, too." My mom gives me a pointed look.

I avoid my mother's stare by looking at Charlotte.

"So, ready to go to work?" my mom asks.

"You bet!" Charlotte answers. "What can we do to help?"

I lead the way to the kitchen, with my mom and Charlotte following and chatting as if they are old friends. I can't help but smile. One parent down, one to go.

After completing last minute preparations for the party, I go in search of my dad. He's hiding out in his garage "workshop," which consists of a small workbench and a handful of tools. He's not much of a handyman, and I suspect it's more of a way to escape. He's tinkering with the lawn mower and drinking a beer while watching the baseball game on a small black and white television.

"Hey, Dad, this is Charlotte, my—" I freeze.

My what? Was it too soon to call her my girlfriend?

"'My girlfriend' is what he is trying to say." She winks in my direction.

I assume Charlotte and my dad exchange pleasantries, but I can't confirm that because all I can hear are her words playing in a loop in my head: *my girlfriend, my girlfriend, my girlfriend.* It is the sweetest song I've ever heard.

The sound of the doorbell ringing breaks my trance.

"Well, I guess we'd better do door duty."

Charlotte and I head into the house, but I steal a quick look back at my dad. He raises his beer in a salute and gives me a smile and a nod. Both parents approve! Nothing can ruin this day.

The party is going along without incident. All of Becky's friends show up—she had been worried her best friend Julia might not make it because she missed school on Friday—and overall there is none of the drama that usually happens when you put a bunch of eight-year-old girls in the same room and then fuel them with cake and ice cream. The girls laugh and play games and ooh and ah over each present my sister opens.

JK shows up about halfway through the party. He's a surprise visitor, and Becky's eyes light up when she sees him. His gift is wrapped as badly as his Christmas present for me had been, but I don't think Becky notices as she tears the paper off. She laughs hysterically when she unveils a five by seven picture of JK with the inscription *From your real brother* written in a permanent marker across the front.

"Best present ever!" JK mimes dropping a microphone.

Becky grins and gives him a hug.

I shake my head. Only JK could get away with that, but I laugh anyway.

"You kill me, JK."

"If I do, I get the girl, right?" He nods his head in Charlotte's direction.

"Still not funny, man."

"Oh, it's funny and you know it. Hey, Charlotte, tell Brian you'd go out with me if he met with an untimely death."

Charlotte counters with, "Oh, there would have to be a lot of untimely deaths before that would happen."

"Oh, that hurts, Charlotte, that hurts me to the core." JK puts one hand to his heart. "And on that painful note, I'm out of here."

"You know she's just kidding," I say.

"Hey, that's my line." He laughs. "Actually, I have a date, so I gotta act like a baby and head on out."

I walk him to the door and go to the kitchen to get a drink for Charlotte. That's when things go south in a hurry.

"Goddamn Phillies," my dad slurs as he stumbles into the kitchen.

My mom frowns "Language, please."

"I wouldn't have to worry about my language if we had a second baseman who could catch a damn ground ball. Two weeks into the season and we're already five out." He searches in the ice box for another beer.

"Haven't you had enough?" my mom asks, lighting the fuse.

My dad glares at her for a long moment, and then explodes.

The next fifteen minutes are a nightmare. My parents engage in the worst shouting match I've ever heard, the volume increasing with each volley of words. In the next room, Charlotte pretends not to notice the yelling while I pretend not to be embarrassed, but neither of us are successful. Becky begins to cry, and her friends try to console her. Then parents arrive, which silences the shouting for the time being but does nothing to stem Becky's tears as they flow down her face. Alarmed moms herd their kids out the door while I stammer out lame excuses about why my sister is upset.

When the kids are finally gone, I try to comfort Becky, but she bursts into a fresh round of tears and retreats to her room. Then it is Charlotte and me and I have nothing to say.

"I guess I should be getting home," she finally says, breaking the awkward silence.

Still no words from me. I mean, what can I say?

She comes closer and whispers in my ear, "Parents fight. It's not a big deal."

Her words help, but she's dead wrong. It is a big deal. My parents had put on an ugly spectacle for everyone to witness. They embarrassed Becky in front of all her friends, and me in front of my girlfriend. It is a huge deal, and I am pissed.

Charlotte gives me a quick squeeze before she leaves, but it feels like a pity hug. Rather than comforting me, it heightens my anger.

And with the last non-family member gone, the shouting starts anew.

Later that night, I pass Becky's bedroom and hear deep heaving sobs followed by gasps of air. I knock softly, and she answers the door. Her eyes are red, and her cheeks are wet with tears. When she sees it's me, she rushes into my arms and holds me. I put my arms around her, and fresh tears flow. I fight back my own, knowing I need to be strong.

"When are they going to stop?"

The yelling has been constant since the party ended, with my parents shouting back and forth in a verbal tennis match. It's past eight o'clock. I wonder if they realize we haven't had dinner.

Another heaving sob from my sister.

"Here, try these." I hand her my earbuds.

I call up a music app on my phone and search for songs Becky might like. The hint of a smile on her face tells me I got it right.

"Is that the Disney station?" she says loudly over the music playing in her ears.

I nod.

She looks at me with an expression of pure love. I show her how to change songs and adjust the volume. We sit on her bed for a long time, with my arm around her and her head on my shoulder, until she drifts off to sleep with *Hakuna Matata* playing in her ears. I lay her head down on the pillow without waking her, pull up the Winnie the Pooh bedspread, and make my way back to my room. With my phone gone, I won't be able to talk to Charlotte or JK, but I figure it's worth it for my sister to get some peace.

April 29

It's been a couple of weeks since my sister's birthday party, and things around the house have been miserable. I came to the growing realization that things with my parents aren't going to get better. There have been days of screaming followed by even worse days of brutal silence. It feels as though this is a new phase in their relationship war, maybe even the end game. My dad spends more and more time at work. When he's home, he broods in front of the TV, with a beer can in one hand and a pall of smoke over his head. My mom puts on a brave face in front of us, but she barely keeps it together most days.

At least Becky has me to lean on, someone she can count on to be there for her. It's a small consolation, but the further apart my parents grow, the closer I get to my sister. She knows I will always be there to listen when she has a problem. It's a one-sided relationship, though. While Becky can unload on me about our parents fighting, the new girl in her class who attracts too much attention, or the myriad other dramatic events happening in the third grade, I can't reciprocate. How can I tell her about my feelings for Charlotte? Would a third grader understand first love?

More importantly, I can't share my deepest secret with her, that, while she sleeps at night, I'm six feet above her head, staring out a window at events that haven't happened yet. I can't tell her I once reached out of that window and pulled back a test while my arm shimmered in and out of existence.

I wake to pouring rain and a stiff wind driving sheets of water against my bedroom window. For a while I lay in my bed and listen to it, thinking the bike ride I had planned with JK is off the table. I haven't seen much of him lately other than at school. It's the downside of having girlfriends, I guess. I think about inviting him over to hang out—I miss sitting around and laughing at his constant stream of quips—but the tension around the house is like a pressure cooker about to blow, and I don't want him to witness a repeat of the birthday party blowup.

The rain continues while I eat my breakfast, a plate of toaster waffles drowned in a pool of syrup.

"I don't know how you can eat those things," my dad says from over his cup of coffee. "Eating the box would be healthier."

I pick up the carton and read through the list of ingredients. "What's not to like here? Enriched flour, eggs, water, vegetable oil. And check out all the vitamins—A, B1, B2, B6, B12. This must have come from the health food aisle."

"Hmm." My dad takes the box. "You missed the 360 milligrams of sodium, the 27 grams of carbohydrates, and the ever-popular beta-carotene for color."

"What's a few carbohydrates among friends?"

"And that's not even counting the lake of syrup. Should we look at the nutrition value for that?"

He reaches for the syrup bottle, but I hold up my hands in defeat. "Okay, okay, you win. It's not the healthiest breakfast."

Becky skips through the kitchen and grabs her raincoat from a hook in the mudroom. "You ready to go, Dad?"

"You bet, Becky. Let's do this." At my puzzled look, he explains, "Your sister and I are going to the mall to get a birthday present for Beth Anne."

"It's Bethany."

"I stand corrected. Your sister and I are going to the mall to get a birthday present for Stephanie."

"Bethany."

"Tiffany?"

"Dad!"

My dad gives me a wink and reaches for his jacket.

My mom is out with friends for coffee, which I imagine is an excuse for them to complain about their husbands. I wonder if my dad has friends to vent to at the office, to relieve the pressure at home. As it is, it's good to see him joking around with Becky and me. I hope it's a sign the tension is easing.

The garage door opens and closes. I run water over my plate and fork and place them in the dishwasher. I put away the syrup and return the half-empty box of toaster waffles to the freezer. With the rain pouring down and a whole Saturday of nothing-to-do in front of me, I do what I am doing more and more these days—I go to the attic.

The attic is filled with light. The view through the octagonal window is of a sunny day, and it takes a few seconds for my eyes to adjust to the brilliance. I'm forced to come to grips with this cloudless sky while I listen to the rain pounding on the roof a few feet above my head. I settle into my chair and, out of the blue, dread fills me. I close my eyes, not wanting to look anymore, but there's no way I can't. I need to know what the window is going to show me.

It's hard to know how far into the future I'm looking. The grass has that mid-summer tinge of brown, and the leaves on the trees appear to be drained of color. Maybe July? Mrs. Goldsmith is weeding in the flowerbox that runs across the front of her house, dropping the weeds into a brown paper bag. The Allen twins toss a bright yellow frisbee back and forth in their front yard. Across the street, Adam Pollock sits in the shade on his front porch reading a comic book and occasionally glancing over at our house.

Does Becky's crush have reciprocal feelings?

One of Adam's fingers pokes into a nostril, and he examines the results of his digging. I turn to see Mrs. Goldsmith looking in his direction. That lady doesn't miss a thing, does she? I look away, feeling guilty for spying on these people's lives, or I guess on what will be their lives in a couple of months. They're oblivious to my presence, while I can see everything they do.

Mrs. Goldsmith pulls a crumpled pack of Marlboro Lights out of the front pocket of her flowered smock, extracts a cigarette, and lights it with a book of matches. She shakes the flame from the match before dropping it into the bag of weeds. As she smokes, she examines the flowerbed, looking for unwanted growth she might have missed. After a moment, she faces the street, and her gaze flicks from house to house as she watches over the neighborhood, searching for anything out of the ordinary she can report to the neighbors over a cup of coffee or later in the day over a bourbon on the rocks.

The Allen twins finish their game of frisbee. Justin tosses the disc toward his front porch while Dustin reaches into his pocket and pulls out car keys. Justin heads for the passenger seat. The twins recently got their driver's licenses and are always looking for an excuse to drive somewhere. The destination is not important—it's the journey they are looking for.

The car starts. It needs a new muffler, and there is mild backfiring when the engine is turned over, which I hear clearly over the rain thrumming on the roof. Across the street, Mrs. Goldsmith scowls in their direction while flicking ash from her cigarette.

Now time slows, and everything is in total clarity.

Coming from my left, passing Mr. Crowley's mailbox, JK rides hell-bent for leather on his bike, with his head down and legs pumping. To my right, Dustin begins backing the car down the driveway. Justin says something, and his brother laughs.

JK is now in front of my house, and he's flying on his bike.

Dustin accelerates down the driveway. JK sees the car. For a split second I think he's going to have enough time to avoid collision. His hands move to the brakes, but his left hand misses the lever, so the back brakes don't engage. In slow motion, the back of the bike lifts off the ground as JK flies over the handlebars. His arms pinwheel helplessly. The bike somersaults, and then it slides along the street before crashing into our brick mailbox. The chain disengages from the gear sprocket and comes to rest in the grass.

JK hits the concrete hard, and his awkward roll carries him to the back of the Allen's driveway, just as Dustin backs the car into the street. The righthand side of the rear bumper smashes into JK's head as he completes his second roll, crushing one side of his polystyrene helmet. His momentum carries him under the rear of the car. Dustin reacts immediately, but instead of the brake, he hits the accelerator. The car smashes JK's legs into the pavement, and he's dragged beneath the undercarriage, leaving a bloody streak that traces the path of the car. The back tires hit the curb across the street, and the rear of the car bounces into the air. The tires regain traction as they hit the grass. Dustin finally finds the brake, mashes the pedal to the floor, and brings the car to a lurching stop on top of the Pollack's azalea bush.

There is complete silence for several seconds as the car comes to a halt. Then the sounds come:

Adam yelling, car doors slamming, a final belch from the muffler, and a single, high-pitched scream. Mrs. Goldsmith lopes awkwardly over from her yard as Dustin and Justin leap from the car. There's confusion as the boys try to figure out what they have hit. Justin notices the shoe, a size eleven sneaker, in the street but doesn't make the connection. It isn't until Dustin checks under the car and sees what's left of JK's body that he realizes what he's done. He turns white and does a final injustice to the azalea bush by puking all over it.

Mrs. Goldsmith is on her cell phone calling 9-1-1 as she waddles toward the car. A look of perverse excitement spreads on her face as she chatters into her phone.

Then Mrs. Allen is out of the house and running across the street, relieved at first to see her boys are unharmed, but her look of relief turns to horror as she learns the truth from Justin. Mrs. Goldsmith has returned to her yard, where a cadre of neighbors wait on her driveway for her to repeat the tale of the car hitting the "crazy black boy on the bike." She relishes her role as the sole eyewitness as the crowd of neighbors grows.

But, unbeknownst to her, I had a perfect view from the attic window.

Everything that happens next is a blur.

My mind keeps reminding me it isn't real, but it doesn't help. After all, the snow wasn't real...until it was. And the tests were real, even though I couldn't find any trace of them later. I just watched JK die, and I know it's going to be real someday, so my brain chooses to shut down.

It's hours later when I step off the attic step into the upstairs hallway. I make my way unsteadily downstairs and grab a soda from the icebox. After a few small sips, I sprint for the bathroom, barely making it to the toilet before puking. I continue to heave until my stomach has nothing left to give. The sickeningly sweet smell of maple syrup hangs in the bathroom even after I flush the remains away.

Exhausted, I curl up on the couch in the living room and fall into a troubled sleep.

May 3

Four days later, I'm reeling over what I saw through the window. I might have been able to better process what I had seen if I had someone to talk to, but that is out of the question. The one person I might have attempted discussing it with would have been JK, but every conversation starter I came up with begins with, "So, I saw you get run over..." and I can't see that going well. I consider telling Charlotte, but she won't believe me, either. Over the next few days, the images fade but don't go completely away. They are the worst at night when I lay awake in bed, staring into the darkness until I drift into a fitful sleep.

I avoid JK at school as much as possible, twice skipping the history class we share and finding excuses to have to run on the other days. I'm sure he notices, but I hope he attributes my actions to being nervous about the upcoming prom, which is partially right. My week is filled with prom preparations—trying on my tux, buying a corsage, and getting a haircut—but mostly worrying about everything that can go wrong that night. And underneath all the things to do is an undercurrent of dread as I remember what I had seen through the window.

May 6

It's my first prom. I stand in front of the bathroom mirror in my rented tuxedo and try repeatedly to get my bow tie to lay straight. It's a losing battle—first the left side rides up, and then the right. My mom takes a turn at it but doesn't fare any better. I give up and go downstairs to pace the kitchen while begging the clock to move faster. Then it's back into the bathroom to check on the status of the ugly pimple on the tip of my nose that chose the worst day to show up. I finally manage to pop it, but it leaves me with an angry red blotch that's even more noticeable. I dab on flesh-colored blemish cream, which helps.

Charlotte is one of three ninth grade girls on the prom court, so I'm feeling extra pressure. Only juniors are eligible to become prom queen but being on the court puts my girlfriend in the royalty class. Feeling like a peasant masquerading as a prince, I look at the clock again, convinced it has stopped.

We're supposed to pick up Charlotte at seven o'clock. "We" being my parents and me. I'm mortified I'm forced to rely on my parents to get me to and from the prom, but I'm not old enough to drive and don't have enough cash to rent a limo for the evening, so my options are limited. My mom is excited because she'll be able to take pictures of the "love birds."

"Promise me you won't say 'love birds' tonight," I implore my mom.

"I'll try, but you two are so cute together."

"Seriously, Mom. I mean it."

75

"Okay, I'm just kidding around with you."

I pause when I hear the words "just kidding." Images of JK being hit by the Allen's car flash into my head, and I shudder.

My mom, who notices everything, tilts her head to one side. "Everything okay, Brian?"

"Yeah, I'm good." But my words don't ring true, and I'm relieved my mom lets my answer stand.

What would I tell her? Sorry, I was thinking about my friend getting crushed under a car in a few months.

I resume my pacing and clock watching.

The time to leave arrives and I'm back in my dad's car, with my sweaty hands clutching the box containing Charlotte's corsage. The flower is something called a Dendrobium Orchid. My mom helped me pick it out at the florist, who suggested something called Baby's Breath to go along with the flower. I don't know anything about flowers except that this one was expensive, and it's purple to match Charlotte's new dress. I'm relieved she suggested a wrist corsage, because the thought of pinning one on her is terrifying.

When we reach Charlotte's driveway, I make one last-ditch attempt to straighten my tie. The curtains in the front window open a couple inches, and I'm pretty sure Charlotte's mom peeks out. I give up on the tie, grab the corsage box, and walk confidently up the walkway, although my insides feel like jelly.

Charlotte's dad opens the front door when I knock. He offers me an extended hand, and we share our typical cold handshake.

"Good evening, sir," I stammer.

"Brian." He nods. "Come on in." He gives a wave to my parents, who are waiting in the car. I look over and see my mom fumbling with the camera case.

Once inside, I don't have to wait long. Charlotte makes her grand entrance down the stairs. It may sound dramatic to say she was making an entrance, but that's what it feels like to me. She flows gracefully down the stairs in her purple dress. A peek of white-strapped shoes appears each time her feet reach for the next step. Her hairdo is done up in a double-braided style that must have taken hours to pull off. Pearl earrings dangle from her ears. That simple walk down the stairs is like watching a princess enter a room to the adoration of her subjects.

"Wow" is all I can come up with. Anything less would have been too understated, and anything more would have come out as incomprehensible blather.

Her smile tells me it was the appropriate response.

Then everyone is in the house. Pictures are taken of me putting the corsage on her wrist, the two of us in front of the fireplace, then sitting on the couch, then back in front of the hearth again. Finally, we make our escape, stopping one final time for a photo op for my mom in front of a large bush. I open the door for Charlotte, and she slides into the backseat. I plop down beside her with all the elegance of a bull in a china shop.

"Thanks for driving us to prom, Mr. and Mrs. Bingham," Charlotte says.

"Oh, we wouldn't have missed it, Charlotte. Your dress is absolutely beautiful, and I love what you did with your hair."

"Thank you so much."

"And what do you think, Brian?" my mom prompts.

"I'm sticking with 'wow.'" I smile, earning me a quick hand squeeze from Charlotte.

The prom is surreal—everything from the decorations to the food and drink to the band is perfect. I walk into the ballroom with the prettiest girl in the room, and I've found enough confidence to own the fact she is with me. The gaze of every guy in the room is on us as Charlotte and I dance. For once, it doesn't bother me. It feels as if we have our own private spotlight following us wherever we go.

"Looking good," JK says as he dances closer to us during a slow song. He's with Tanya Miller, a junior on the prom court. He and Brittany broke up a couple of weeks ago—both claiming they were the one who initiated the breakup—but my friend hadn't had any problem in finding a replacement. The cheerleading captain, no less.

"Thanks, man."

"Not you, moron." He nods toward Charlotte.

"I look good because of my date." She smiles.

"Are you talking about this guy with the crooked tie?"

Charlotte pauses to straighten my tie. "Yes, that's my guy." She kisses me on the cheek.

"I guess there's no accounting for taste." He grins as he twirls Tanya away from us.

I stare into Charlotte's eyes, totally smitten with this beautiful, perfect person holding onto me in the middle of a dance floor.

* * *

The crowd cheers wildly. Tanya has been announced as the prom queen. JK is practically preening in front of the stage as the principal puts the crown on Tanya's head. You would have thought it was him being crowned. Tanya gives an exaggerated royal wave, and everyone erupts into laughter.

"Yeah, Tanya," JK yells, pumping his fist in the air.

I applaud in support even though I don't know her—Tanya's clique of friends run in air people like me are unlikely to ever breathe. I'm amazed JK was able to score a date with her, and to prom no less, the ultimate event of the high school year. Sure, he cuts a fine figure in his tuxedo. Sure, his dance moves are phenomenal, nothing at all like the robotic steps I take, but there's more to it. I mean, here's a guy who has been passed from foster home to foster home for the past eight years. He's got no real family, other than mine. He doesn't wear the best clothes or drive a fancy car. Yet here he is, stepping out with the prom queen, all the while believing it's exactly where he should be.

JK and I watch as Tanya dances with Rich Matton, the newly crowned prom king. Rich is the quarterback of the football team, which makes him the bluest of the blue bloods in any high school. Apart from Charlotte, the prom court is all cheerleaders and football players. I don't know what it's about high school football—especially our team, which had a two and nine record for the season—but for some reason it automatically launches you into the social stratosphere. Even the guys who didn't play were treated with deference, especially on game days when they strutted around in their jerseys. In the meantime, guys like Brendon Thomas were shunned. All he did was score a perfect thirty-six on his ACT test, a feat that will likely get him into his choice of Ivy League schools. The most one of these football jocks can hope for is to work for Brendon someday. And it isn't only the smart kids who are passed over. Even Jack Lindrom, a sophomore who took first in the state in wrestling for the past two years, and Mike Tremain, the ace pitcher and leading hitter on the baseball team, didn't make the cut when it came to the "in crowd." It's football players and cheerleaders... and then everyone else.

Midway through the coronation song, the rest of the prom court joins in the dance. Charlotte's partner is a freshman linebacker named Nick Baines. He made it into two games the entire season, but here he is on the dance floor, holding my girlfriend too closely.

"What an asshole," I mumble to JK.

"Being a lousy linebacker doesn't make him an asshole."

"No, but dancing with my girlfriend does."

"It's tradition, man."

"Screw tradition. Why do they have to play a slow song? I don't like the way his hand keeps sliding down her back."

JK nods but doesn't respond. I don't think I've ever seen JK get angry about anything. Nothing ever fazes him. He always says he's like a duck; water rolls right off him.

The song finally ends, and the dancers separate. Nick gives Charlotte a quick hug, and I'm glad to see she doesn't reciprocate. I stare at Nick with an angry scowl, but he laughs and gestures with one hand as if to say, "come on, man, let's have a go if you want to." I start to step forward, ready to do just that, when JK grabs my arm.

"That's half the football team out there," he warns.

"I don't care."

JK takes my shoulders and turns me so he can look at my face. "Hey, Brian, you know I'm with you if you think this needs to happen, but we'll probably get our asses kicked."

The thought of JK being willing to stand by me when we have no chance is enough to make me rethink what I'm about to do. I take a deep breath and drop back a step. Nick laughs it up with a couple other guys from the football team.

JK puts an arm around my shoulders and walks me toward Charlotte. "Good choice, man."

"What was that all about?" Charlotte asks. "I don't know what was going on, but it was very un-Brian like behavior."

"I was defending my territory," I reply tersely.

"Territory? Is that what I am, territory?"

"Sorry, that didn't come out right, I guess."

"You guess right," she says with a touch of ice in her voice.

The next few minutes pass in uncomfortable silence as I stand next to Charlotte and pretend to watch the packed dance floor. Anything I say will come out defensive, so I decide saying nothing is my best course of action. Charlotte excuses herself to go to the restroom, and I stand at one side of the room. JK and Tanya are dancing to a fast song, twirling and bobbing to the beat. It's the kind of song that would showcase my poor dancing skills, so I'm half glad Charlotte's not here.

When she returns, I move to make things right.

"Hey, I'm really sorry, Charlotte. I guess I got jealous watching you dance with that jerk."

She gives me a long look before responding. "Brian, have I given you a reason to believe I was interested in anyone else?"

"No, it's just that you could go out with anyone you wanted to."

"Maybe, but I'm choosing to go out with you."

I start to speak, but there's no sense in digging a bigger hole than the one I've already dug. Instead, I open my arms and pull her in for a long hug.

A song starts, thankfully a slow one, and we turn our hug into a slow dance.

The rest of the prom goes by uneventfully, but that changes as Charlotte and I walk hand in hand out of the ballroom and run into Nick Baines and a small band of freshman football players. The smell of alcohol is strong on Nick's breath as he steps forward to block our way.

"You got a problem with me, Bingham?" He slurs his words, and I wonder how much he's had to drink.

"Let it go, Brian," Charlotte whispers, and I'm prepared to do that as I start to brush past him, but I don't make it to the door before two of Nick's teammates slide into our path.

"You always let your girlfriend talk for you?" Nick taunts.

I turn to face him as Charlotte puts a hand on my arm.

"I'm not looking for trouble, Nick," I say in a calm voice.

"Well, shit, you found it anyway." He laughs as he gives me a shove.

I manage to maintain my composure. I offer up a tight-lipped smile as I take Charlotte by the hand and turn toward the exit, but Nick isn't done with me yet.

"After you drop off your girl, I guess you'll be headed over to your loser friend JK's house for a sausage party, huh?"

Something inside of me snaps, and I spin around. I'm on Nick before he can react. I throw two wild punches, one that clips his shoulder and another finding nothing but air. Nick gapes at me in surprise before stepping forward and burying a fist in my stomach. I bend over, gasping for air and trying not to throw up. Nick follows up the gut shot with a punch that hits me dead center in the face, crushing my lips into my teeth. I drop to one knee as Charlotte gasps and Nick's friends laugh.

"Nice one, Nick!" someone yells, maybe Tony Gregorio, but I can't be sure as I'm trying to deal with my mouth filling with blood. I spit out a red glob of spit, half-heartedly aiming for Nick's shoes. I glance down, and I'm relieved to see there isn't a tooth floating in the splatter of blood on the ground.

Charlotte kneels by my side as Nick and his friends leave in a chorus of laughter and high-fives.

"Are you okay, Brian?"

I suck in air through my nose and turn my head to let loose another stream of blood and spittle from my mouth. I bit into my tongue when Nick punched me, and it isn't going to stop bleeding anytime soon.

"Yeah, never better," I mumble.

The rest of my prom night consists of rinsing out my mouth with cold water until the bleeding finally stops. Nick's punch cut my lips, which swell up and turn a shade of purple within minutes. Everything I say comes out as a mumble, so I quit trying to speak. My nose is swelling, and in the bathroom mirror I see my eyelids already beginning to blacken. It's hard to believe one punch, even perfectly placed, could do that much damage to a face.

Charlotte sticks with me throughout, but she isn't happy with me throwing the first punches, feeble as they might have been. Even if I could speak clearly, she won't understand I was defending my friend, who has months to live if the window is right.

In retrospect, if I was going to take the blame for the fight, I wish I had at least done some damage to that smug asshole.

The prom ends with a silent ride home and me staring at the reflection of my stupid crooked tie in the passenger window of my dad's car. I occasionally reach up to dab at my swollen lip with a bloody napkin.

Charlotte is right. It was un-Brian like behavior. I wanted to blame stress, and there is no doubt I've got plenty of that with my parents' constant fighting, worrying about my grades, and my ongoing fear of losing Charlotte. The argument and fight certainly wasn't going to help with that last concern.

But if I'm honest with myself, none of that had anything to do with what happened tonight. It was the window, the window and the horrific event I'd seen through its polished octagon frame four days ago.

It had to do with watching my best friend dragged across the street under a car. It had to do with him dying right before my eyes.

"Want to talk about it?" my dad asks as we pull out of Charlotte's driveway after dropping her off. A goodnight kiss was off the table, and even her brief hug felt cold.

"Not really."

"Would ice cream help?" Ice cream is my dad's solution for most of the bad things that have happened in my life.

"Not this time."

"I don't know. The cold could reduce the swelling."

After a long pause, I decide ice cream couldn't make the situation worse, and it probably *would* feel good on my swollen lips. My dad drives to Zeke's Concretes, a local favorite. We don't speak on the way, and I consider telling him to skip it and head for home when I see tuxedos and fancy prom dresses in the waiting line. That's the last thing I need.

My dad also notices and asks, "How about we go through the drive-thru?"

"Yeah, good call."

I slink down in my seat as my dad orders and pulls out of the parking lot. We sit in the car in our driveway, finishing off the ice cream before we go into the house. I'm careful not to drop my chocolate marshmallow concrete on my tux. I don't need any more problems. The ice cream does feel good on my lips, and when I prod gingerly with my finger it feels like the swelling may be going down a bit.

"Did you at least get in a couple of your own punches?" my dad asks.

"Not hardly. A shot to the shoulder and a big swing and a miss."

"Well, I bet he won't be able to move his shoulder for a week."

I smile even though it hurts to do it.

"You know I had to do it, don't you, Dad?"

He waits patiently for me to go on. I don't quite know where to go, though. Telling him about the window is out, but I guess I could tell him what set me off.

"JK doesn't have family but me, you know?"

My dad nods but remains silent.

"And family always sticks up for each other, right?"

Another nod.

"That's why I had to do it."

My dad looks over at me. "If you had to do it again, knowing the possible consequences, would you do it again?"

Without hesitation, I answer "Yes."

"Well, then, I'd say you did the right thing."

I lean over and give my dad an uncharacteristic hug.

As I lay in bed that night, I think about the first time JK had come to my rescue. In the sixth grade, I weighed seventy pounds soaking wet. To make matters worse, I'd made the unwise decision to choose the clarinet as my instrument for band. While the other boys were noisily banging away on their percussion instruments or blasting air into tubas and trumpets, I was playing lilting and squeaky melodies with the six girls who had also chosen the clarinet. To say I was a number one target for the bullies in middle school would be an understatement.

I tried to avoid confrontation, even if it meant taking the back hallway to class to avoid the older kids, but one afternoon I found myself pushed against a fence by Hank Jackson, the biggest eighth-grader at Hamilton Middle School.

"What's your problem, Brian?" he asked, clearly playing to the small crowd of students making their way from the soccer field back into the school. Hoots and whistles filled the air. A threatening look from Hank silenced the crowd, and he turned his attention back to me. "Well?"

I wanted to tell him my immediate problem was trying to breathe with his hand wrapped tightly around my throat, but I didn't think it was the answer he was looking for. My gaze swept frantically left and right, seeking out a teacher, but Hank had chosen an area out of the line of sight of the school building. I watched helplessly as Mark Watson picked up my clarinet case and heaved it over the fence into a bush.

The bell signaling the next period rang, but no one made a move toward the school. I guess it was worth a detention for being late to class if they could witness a sixth grader get his butt kicked. Without releasing his chokehold, Hank raised a fist, and I closed my eyes.

"That's pretty impressive, Hank. Damn, I wish I could beat up someone half my size."

Recognizing, JK's voice, I opened my eyes.

Hank dropped his fist and released his hand from my throat. I sank back against the fence and rubbed my neck, sucking in large gulps of air as I watched the confrontation unfolding before me. Hank turned slowly toward JK. His face reddened in fury. My friend was a good fifty pounds lighter and six inches shorter than Hank, but that didn't matter to JK. He stood face to face with Hank, staring up into Hank's eyes.

"Kick his ass, Hank!" a voice called from the crowd, prompting more cackles from the others.

"This doesn't involve you, punk," Hank said.

"Actually, it does," JK responded.

"And why is that?"

"Because Brian is my friend."

"Is he a good enough friend to get your ass

kicked?" Hank threatened.

JK took his time to answer the question. He looked at me and then back at Hank. A small smile came to his face. "Yeah, I guess he is."

"You think I'm just kidding?"

"That's my line," JK said.

That was enough for Hank. He shoved JK; his two large paw-like hands landing squarely on JK's shoulders. JK flew back against the fence but managed to keep his balance.

"Still think it's funny?" Hank jeered.

"No, but the principal might." JK smiled again.

"Well, Principal Dickhead isn't here, is he?"

"No, but Principal Dickson is," came a deep voice.

Hank dropped his fists and turned to see the principal standing behind him.

"Let's take a walk to my office to discuss this, Harold."

The crowd roared when the principal called Hank by his real name.

"And the rest of you can follow us to pick up your detention slips for being late to class," he said, silencing the laughter.

The crowd trailed behind the principal, leaving JK and me standing alone.

I started to thank him, but JK held up his hand.

"It's what friends do, man."

Two weeks following the fence incident, Hank and a couple of his thug buddies caught JK behind the gym and tore into him. He sustained two cracked ribs courtesy of kicks delivered by Hank's steel-toed boots, but JK never let out a whimper during the beating. He told me later it was worth it.

Years later, it was my turn. I got my butt kicked, but JK was right. It was worth it.

May 4

I wake feeling groggy. My lips throb and stick together with dried blood. I dampen a washcloth with warm water and moisten my lips until I can finally get them to separate. I carefully wash off as much of the dried blood as I can. My tongue seeks out the cuts, and I grimace in pain. I down a couple of aspirin with a gulp of water. The reflection looking back at me in the mirror is grotesque. My lips are bloody and swollen to twice their normal size. My eyelids are black. The left side of my face has a purple-yellow bruise from my jawline all the way to my eye. I pull up my T-shirt and see exactly where Nick's first punch landed. There's a nice welt surrounded by more bruising. I touch it gingerly. Painful but not as sore as my face.

I check my phone and see Charlotte has texted me. *How are you feeling?*

I respond. *I'm not as pretty as usual, but I'll survive.*

I think to myself that JK would've been proud of my comeback. I consider sending Charlotte a selfie of my battered face, but I don't see how it's going to buy me anything other than sympathy. It's not like I got my butt kicked defending her, and I technically started the fight by throwing the first punches.

"Hey, Brian, your dad's at work and Becky and I are headed to the mall, okay?" my mom calls from the bottom of the stairs.

"Sure," I yell back. Even that one syllable comes out muddled through my swollen lips.

"Bye, Brian," Becky yells.

The garage door goes up and back down again. Then there is silence in the house.

I'm considering going back to bed but notice my pillowcase has several large bloodstains on it. My sheet has a couple of spots, too, so I strip my bed and drop the linens in the washing machine. I dump in an extra cup of detergent for good measure, but I may have to throw the pillowcase away later.

My stomach feels queasy, so I pass on breakfast, opting for a large glass of ice water. I take small sips, letting the cold water linger on my lips. With no one around, I venture up into the attic. The view out of the window is undulating eddies of gray. I undo the latch, and the window opens silently on its tiny hinges. The fog moves eagerly through the opening, reaching for me. I close my eyes and let it swirl around me.

As the fog engulfs my head, there's a tingling feeling, like tiny electric shocks moving in waves from one side of my scalp to the other. I jerk my head out of the fog and the sensation stops. I tentatively dip my head back into the gray and the tingling begins again. The shocks are not painful, but they make it is impossible to concentrate. Thoughts and images flicker in and out of my head with no clear pattern. Odors appear, honeysuckle mixed with a darker smell of rot. Tastes move across my tongue, not discernable flavors but more the sensation of saltiness, sweetness, and something foul that causes my queasy stomach to clench. It reminds me of a classroom experiment we did in science class—something about mapping the taste buds, but I can't focus on the memory long enough for it to become clear. Sounds appear from far away, ghostly and otherworldly. I try to concentrate, to give the sounds meaning, but my thoughts have already moved on.

The fog caresses my face, and a tendril slides

down into my T-shirt. Something tells me I need to pull out of the fog, but my thoughts are interrupted by swirling images of color and a droning buzz that sounds like a chorus of muffled voices. I struggle to make out the words, but my taste buds are overwhelmed with the cloying flavor of caramel and something else, something coppery—is that blood?

I yank my head from the fog. The last ghostly fingers cling for purchase while I push against the window. I manage to get it closed and secured. My thoughts clear, as does the view through the window. I look out on my slice of the world through the octagonal glass—a typical spring day bordering on the edge of summer, with kids playing and dads pushing lawnmowers through the grass. I look down at the latch and wonder if that tiny piece of hardware will to be able to contain the fog if it wanted to come into the attic. Will I be able to stop it?

I retreat from the attic and go back to my room. I take a quick glance at my phone and see it's blown up with text messages, four from Charlotte, one from my dad, three from JK, and another dozen from friends who want to know how badly I got my ass kicked. I check the time and see it's three o'clock.

That can't possibly be right.

I look again to see I read it right the first time. I was in the attic for five hours. That explains why I'm starving. Before heading downstairs for food, I stop off in the bathroom to take a leak. I look in the mirror on my way to the toilet and stop dead in my tracks.

The bruise on my face is gone. The coloring around my eyes is back to normal. My lips are no longer swollen, and there's no sign of any cuts. I lift my T-shirt and the discoloration is gone, too. It's like the punches never happened.

I guess I shouldn't be surprised, but it doesn't stop the wave of dizziness that comes over me when

I face my reflection. Even when I lean in to within a couple of inches from the mirror, there's no sign I had been in a fight. No cuts, no discoloration, nothing. Even the untimely zit is gone.

When I pull my bed linens from the washing machine, the bloodstains have vanished. Either that extra cup of detergent did the trick, or...

Or what? The magic window has more powers than I thought?

I blow off most of the texts but spend a few minutes on the ones I care about. I return the text from my dad. I assure him I'm okay and send him a selfie of my newly repaired face to prove it. That might be one I'll have to explain later since he was a witness to how banged-up I was last night. I have a quick text conversation with JK. He heard about the fight. I'm not surprised—based on the number of texts I've received it's been a major topic of post-prom conversation. I tell him I'm fine and send the obligatory *LOL* when he asks me if I need a bad-ass dude to come to my rescue. When my chat with JK peters out, I turn my attention to Charlotte's texts. She's concerned about me, which makes me feel good since we'd had a couple of tense moments the night before. I send her a selfie with a thumbs up and a big grin on my face to assure her everything is fine.

She responds, *Wow! Not a mark on you!*

I reply with something lame about the Bingham family being fast healers and then tell her I've got to catch up on reading for History. I feel bad about lying, but what choice do I have? She wouldn't believe me if I told her the truth.

Although I do have reading I should be doing, homework is the last thing on my mind. All I can think about is the window and the healing powers of the mysterious fog. I come to grips with the fact there is something in the fog that healed my cuts and bruises. I wish I could bottle that stuff. Dr. Bingham Wonder-Cure could make me a millionaire overnight. Hell, if all it could do was cure pimples, it was worth its weight in gold.

May 11

I'm back in the attic, staring out of the window into the darkness. I've been up here every night this week, sometimes for a few minutes but usually for a couple of hours. I keep wondering when my parents are going to say something about me being up here so much, but they have more important things on their minds. There's nothing going on outside the window tonight apart from a car or two passing by. The faint glow of a firefly flickers. Across the street, Mrs. Goldsmith's curtains part, and her round face peers out of the darkness for a few seconds before the drapes are drawn again.

The window is a clear pane of glass tonight, but twice this week the view was nothing but fog. On both occasions, I unlatched the tiny gold clasp and opened the window a few inches, hypnotized by the shifting tendrils of vapor as they made their way through the opening. It was like tiny fingers reaching in, learning how far they could extend their presence into the room. I had been afraid of the fog at first, but now it's a comforting presence. When I extend my hand toward the cloud, an immediate sense of peace falls over me. I forget about my parents fighting as the fog's ghostly fingers stretch to touch mine.

When I'm in contact with the fog, the tiny electric shocks—what I call "head buzzies"—move across the top of my scalp in waves. I welcome the respite from thinking about everything going on in my life and give in to the incoherence. When I pull away, the tingling stops, and my thoughts become clear once again. More and more, though, I find myself touching the fog for longer periods of time. The numbing of my brain helps me to forget what will happen to JK.

But what price am I paying for the temporary relief?

I have to tell JK.

May 17

"Have you ever thought about what happens when we die?"

JK looks up at me in surprise. Even though we're best friends, we didn't often engage in anything resembling a serious conversation. He nabs a couple of fries from my plate as he thinks about my question.

"No, I can't say that I have," he said.

I nod in silence while he looks at me with a raised eyebrow. I take another bite of my burger as I think about how to proceed now that I've opened up the topic of death.

"Would you want to know ahead of time?" I ask.

"What, when I'm going to die?"

"Yeah, would you want to know?"

"I guess not. Unless there was something I could do to prevent it, of course."

I bought myself some more time by slowly wiping my mouth with a napkin. I have no idea if there is a way to prevent his death. I only know the snow happened, the tests were real, and my bruises disappeared. The window is batting a thousand so far.

"Is there something you know that I don't, Nostradamus?" he asks. He takes a couple more fries from my plate while he grins across the table at me.

I open my mouth to tell him about the window, but I chicken out.

"The only thing I know is that I'm going to kick your ass if you take one more fry."

"Yeah?" JK slowly reaches over, takes a fry, and methodically swirls it in my ketchup. "How'd that last fight go for you?"

13

May 23

Becky and I are walking back from the movie theater on Saturday afternoon when the moving van passes us. *Two Men and a Truck* is painted on the side. A muscular guy in a tight-fitting, black T-shirt has one tattooed arm hanging out the passenger side window—skulls and flowers and Chinese characters in various colors. The right rear tire is low on air. I know, even before it passes, *WASH ME* will be etched into the dirt on the back of the truck. It rumbles past, and my fears are confirmed. It's the same truck I'd seen through the attic window months ago.

Becky continues to ramble on about the movie, but my thoughts are on what I will find when we get home. What's in the truck? Where is it headed?

From four houses away, I see my mom's minivan and my dad's Accord parked in the driveway, but the Blue Bomb is gone. The Blue Bomb is my dad's 1962 Ford Falcon, a boxy clunker that might have been blue at one time but has faded into a lifeless gray. The plastic upholstery is torn, exposing chunks of faded yellow foam. The plastic steering wheel is enormous, the radio doesn't work, and the windshield wipers run on a vacuum pump—the faster you go, the slower the wipers run, making it impossible to drive more than twenty miles an hour when it's raining. The rear passenger window has a large gray strip of duct tape running diagonally across the window to keep a crack from spreading. It's embarrassing to be seen in the car, but my dad loves it. And he's saving it for me for when I turn sixteen. I can't imagine the horror of pulling up in front of Charlotte's house to pick her up for a date in that monstrosity. I can already feel her father's judgement. Would he even allow his daughter to ride in something that looked as if it was held together by rust?

"Dad must be out driving the Bomb," Becky says as we reach the driveway.

"Yeah," I respond, suspecting something much worse.

Becky returns to her movie commentary, but I'm no longer paying attention.

Across the street, Mrs. Goldsmith and Mrs. Allen continue their conversation. When I look over, Mrs. Allen drops her gaze to the ground, refusing to meet my eyes. Mrs. Goldsmith lowers her voice but has no problem staring directly at me when I look in her direction.

Mom is smoking and staring out the back window at nothing when I enter the house. Her eyes are red and the hand holding her cigarette shakes as she turns toward us.

"Where's Daddy?" Becky asks, but I already know.

Mom confirms it when she says, "Have a seat, guys. We need to have a talk."

Becky pulls out a kitchen chair and sits, but I remain standing. From my vantage point, I can see into the living room. Dad's chair, the one he always sits in to watch TV, is gone, as is the round side table that holds his ash tray and a set of coasters from a long-ago vacation to Maine. He forgot to use the coasters most of the time and the table has water rings from where he would rest a cold beer. My mom used to nag him about using the coasters, but I guess that isn't going to happen anymore.

"Dad's gone, isn't he?" I ask. I look directly at my

mom, daring her to refute my statement.

"Yes." Straightforward, not trying to pull the wool over my eyes or even soften the blow.

Becky looks confused. "Gone where?"

"Don't you get it, Becky? Dad moved out."

Becky stares at my mom, imploring her to set me straight, but my mom remains silent as she takes another drag from her cigarette and exhales the smoke out of her nose. She's too exhausted to even reply.

Finally, she nods, "Your dad and I have decided we need time apart."

"Time apart? What does that mean?" Becky asks as tears well in her eyes.

"He's moving into an apartment," Mom says and quickly adds when she sees my reaction, "but you'll get to see him whenever you want."

"Well, at least we won't have to put up with the yelling all the time." I turn and stomp out of the room.

"Brian—"

I continue up the stairs to my room. I slam the door and sink back onto my bed. I stare at the ceiling as a horrible thought courses through my head.

I'm devastated my father moved out, but that's not what I can't stop thinking about. The window had foretold the moving van, all the way down to *Wash Me* written in the grime on the rear door. I don't need anything more to convince me the window is legit.

That means it's a matter of time before JK dies in that horrible accident.

That presents me with a dilemma. Should I try again to tell him? Not that he would believe me anyway—it's crazy to think anyone would buy into the story of a magical window that can show you the future. Oh, and as a side benefit, it's great at curing what ails you.

Assuming he would believe me, would he even

want to know? Would he change anything in his life? There's a Tim McGraw song about a guy who finds out he is dying from cancer and does crazy things like skydiving and riding a bull. Would JK want to do that? I picture JK climbing onto the back of a thousand-pound bull, but I can't wrap my head around that.

My dad used to buy lottery tickets when the jackpot got up to a couple hundred million dollars. Even though he knew the odds of winning were close to zero, he told me he imagined what he would do with the money.

"After taxes, you'd be looking at eighty million in the bank," he would tell me. "Even if I give twenty of it to family and twenty to charity, that leaves us with forty million, Brian. Forty million dollars! Do you know how that would change our lives?"

"But you know you're not going to win, right, so why even dream about it?" I'd ask.

"Because that's the beauty of not knowing what's coming around the bend, Son. In one version of the future, I'm the guy posing for the picture with one of those ridiculously large checks, and for the next twenty-four hours, I can live in that future."

* * *

I call Charlotte to tell her the news of my parents splitting up. Having someone to share it with makes the load lighter.

"Do you want to come over to talk about it?" she asks with concern in her voice.

"Can you come over here, instead?" There's a plan forming in the back of my head.

I need to know something, not that it will change anything, but I need to know anyway. Am I the only one who can see out of the window? I need to know because I've been thinking about my dad's lottery tickets and his version of the future. I'm hoping someone else's rendering of the future will be different than mine. Maybe in that version, JK doesn't die in front of my house. In that alternate universe, we could marry Tanya and Charlotte, live down the street from each other, have kids who are best friends, and grow old and fat, brothers to the end. Hell, my dad could end up winning the lottery, too. Wouldn't that be a nice future?

Is it possible? I need to find out.

I'm waiting on the front porch when Charlotte arrives thirty minutes later. She gives me a long hug, and for a minute the world is right again—well, not exactly right again, but at least manageable. I take her hand and lead her up the stairs to my room, glancing up as we pass under the cord dangling down from the attic opening.

We talk in my room for the next hour. Charlotte, who usually leads our conversations, mostly listens as I let it all out.

"It kills me to see them going at each other all the time," I say, staring down at the carpet because I'll break into tears if I look at her. "Every damn day is like a war. I don't even know who to blame anymore."

"Sometimes no one is to blame, Brian," Charlotte whispers, with her arm resting on my shoulder.

"If they hated each other that much, why did they even get married in the first place?"

"Sometimes things don't work out as we plan."

"Yeah, tell me about it."

"You know what I think?" Charlotte asks.

I look at her for the first time since we entered my room.

"I think your parents loved each other very much. They probably still do. Sometimes life gets in the way, little things get in the way, and then the little things become big things. You don't even see it coming. No one can. We can't see into the future."

Oh, but some of us can, Charlotte. Some of us

99

can, and the future isn't pretty.

Her comment about the future brings me back to the present. I steer the conversation to my childhood, and from there to family vacations, which segues nicely to family photo albums stored, conveniently, in the attic.

Charlotte scrutinizes the pine ladder I've pulled from the ceiling. "Are you sure these stairs are safe?"

"If they'll hold me, they can hold you." I scamper up the stairs and pull myself through the hatchway. I look back down and extend a hand, but she is already halfway up. The attic is lit with bright sunlight streaming through the window.

"Is there a light?" she asks when she reaches the top of the stairs.

I start to say something, but then the truth sinks in. The attic is dark because she can't see the window. I walk to the center of the room and pull the string to turn on the light.

"You may find this hard to believe, but this is my first time in an attic," Charlotte says, stepping tentatively onto the plywood floor. "It's safe to walk on this floor, right?"

I take her hand and walk her past the stacks of Christmas decorations. We stand in front of the window. Outside, Adam Pollack rides past the house on his bike. Mrs. Goldsmith peers out from behind the front drapes and squints her eyelids while making sure her young neighbor isn't up to mischief. I look at Charlotte in anticipation, but she doesn't react.

"Nice view from up here, don't you think?" I ask.

"I guess, if you like to look at boxes," she says, eyeing me strangely. "So, where are the photo albums?"

I point toward a stack of cardboard boxes. We rummage through them and end up finding a couple of albums we take back down to my room. Charlotte laughs at pictures of me when I was Becky's age.

"You were so cute," she gushes.

My face burns, and she laughs.

She turns the page and pictures of brilliant autumn foliage are captured inexpertly through the lens of a cheap camera. Despite that, the photos are stunning.

"Wow, these are amazing. Where were you?"

"I guess this was on our trip to Maine," I reply, looking at the pictures as though it's the first time I've seen them. Truth be told, I don't recall much about the vacation. All I remember is my dad kept pulling to the side of the road so my mom could take pictures of the fall foliage. Then my dad would drive on until my mom had him pull over at another spot that looked identical to the last one. We'd all hop out of the car while she took more pictures. To an eight-year-old, the repeated exercise grew boring, so after the first couple of times, I didn't bother getting out of the car. I stayed in the back and read comic books. My sister slept through it all, purring softly in her car seat.

For me, the one highlight of the trip was getting to go up in a working lighthouse. While ascending the winding staircase, the stairs grew narrower as we neared the top, so my dad had to duck his head. The final ten feet to the top were gained by climbing a steel ladder, where we emerged through an opening into the small room containing the rotating light. The view of the ocean from the top of the structure was amazing, with the pounding waves crashing into the rocks on the shore a hundred and fifty feet below me.

As she flips through the photo album, Charlotte provides ongoing commentary about the brilliant golds and reds set amongst the green of the pines and the rugged, desolate seascapes.

I think about the coasters my mom bought during that trip and how my dad didn't ever put his beer can on top of them. I think about the view from the lighthouse and about my family being happy. But mostly, I think about how Charlotte didn't see the window.

My desperate thoughts of alternate futures go out the window.

May 25

JK takes my parents' breakup hard. He gives me an uncharacteristic hug when I open the door.

"I don't have the words, man," he says.

"Thanks."

"You know I'd do anything for you, don't you?"

I nod, unable to hold back tears.

We hang out in my room for a while, not saying much. And that's okay. Sometimes just knowing someone is there for you is better than any words that could be spoken. I finally break the long silence.

"There's something I've got to tell you."

JK opens his mouth to reply but sees the look on my face and closes it again.

"You're going to think I'm going crazy," I start. I pause to take deep breath. "And maybe you'd be right."

JK shifts his position on the beanbag chair and gives me his full attention.

I tell him everything—the window, the snow, the tests, the moving van. He looks skeptical but lets me continue before weighing in.

"But that's not the worst of it." Another deep breath. "I also saw you get run over by a car."

"Wait...what? You saw me get hit by a car?"

I nod. "Not just hit. You get run over and killed."

JK looks closely at my face, trying to see if I am messing with him. My look must have told him otherwise.

"Show me," he said.

"Show you what?"

"The window. Show it to me." He rises from the beanbag chair.

"But I'm not sure if you'll be able to see it. Charlotte..."

"Show me." He is already heading out of my room.

I catch up to him in the hallway. I look up at the cord. It is swaying slowly as it dangles from the attic steps.

"Is that it?" JK asks. I nod.

JK reaches up and pulls the ladder from the ceiling. He scrambles up the steps. He pokes his head through the hatchway.

"Is there a light up here?"

"Yeah, there's a bulb with a pull chain."

His footsteps clomp across the wood floor as I climb the ladder. The light flashes on and the attic is illuminated. When I pull myself through the hatchway, JK is closely examining each wall. My heart sinks as he walks right by the window. He turns and looks at me. I can't tell if he's angry or just confused.

"I got nothing, man," he says. "There's no window up here. Is this some kind of joke? If you're about to say Just Kidding, I'll remind you that it's my line."

"I'm not kidding, JK."

"Then I don't get it. There's no window in this attic."

I walk over to the window. I look out and see everything in front of my house. There's JK's bike leaning up against a tree, his helmet hanging from one handlebar. If he can't see the window, I must look like I am staring at drywall, but I don't know how to explain it to him.

JK is already climbing down the steps. I pull the chain to extinguish the bulb. I can still see perfectly well with the light from the window. I climb down after my friend and release the steps back into the ceiling.

JK stands in the hallway and looks at me closely.

"Hey, I know you're going through a lot right now," he says.

"Yeah, but..."

"There's no window, Brian. You should try to get some rest, man."

There's nothing I can say that will convince him, so I just shrug my shoulders. "Yeah, you're probably right," I reply.

"On the positive side," he says, "It looks like I'm not going to die anytime soon so I guess you're stuck with having this bad ass dude as your best friend."

I smile, but my heart isn't behind it.

May 28

With the ringing of the three o'clock bell, I've officially made it through my freshman year. I close my dented locker for the last time, leaving a stack of random papers and loose pens and pencils for its next owner. I guess it won't truly be "official" until I get my report card in a few weeks, but I feel better about my grades. I did have help from the window, of course, but mostly the improvement in my grades was due to me putting in the work to study, despite juggling everything else going on in my life.

Stuff is piling up—good and bad. On the bad side, there are a couple of biggies. My parents' weeklong separation is too new for me to have fully internalized yet, but it's a constant weight on me. Mom is merely going through the motions. Dinner last night was cereal because she said she didn't have the energy to cook. She smokes and stares out of the window a lot. Over the weekend, I saw her looking through the want ads in the newspaper. She circled a few opportunities with a red pen before throwing the entire section in the trash can a few minutes later.

My sister sits in front of the television at night, clutching her favorite stuffed animal, a purple unicorn my dad won for her at the state fair when she was four years old. It had been her constant companion for years before she gave it up when she entered second grade. "I'm too old for stuffed animals," she'd stated at the time, relocating them to the top shelf of her closet. Now all the animals are back on her bed, and the unicorn is in its familiar place under her arm.

And then there's the vision of JK's horrible death. This is the worst of my current problems. Not that my parents living in two different places isn't horrible, but at least there's a chance they'll get back together. With JK, there's no hope for a different outcome other than what I have already seen from the window. Worse, I can't prepare for it. Every day may be his last. And when that day finally comes, it will be my fault because I haven't done enough to stop it from happening. This guilt hangs over me like a cloud.

Even my girlfriend is complicated. My relationship with Charlotte couldn't be going better, at least in my estimation, and I guess that's where the problem lies. I hope she feels the same, but I doubt it. I still can't figure out why she's going out with me when she could have anyone she wants. Other guys stare as we walk through the hallways, or at the mall, or down the street. Their expressions say, "What is she doing with him?" And I don't have a good answer. I worry I'm spending too much time with her, or not enough, or saying the wrong thing, or not speaking up when I should.

My parents, my sister, my girlfriend, my best friend—that's too much to take on at once. Most days I hold it together, but in the middle of the night when I'm wide awake, pictures spin through my head. Charlotte with another guy. My parents in divorce court. My teachers finding out I cheated on my tests. Becky crying in her bedroom. The bloody skid mark where JK's body was dragged across the street. Over and over the images come, faster and faster until they become a blur and I awake, drenched in sweat and clutching my pillow.

On the nights when I can't sleep because of my racing thoughts, I climb into the attic. Even if the view is nothing more than the washed-out yellow light on Mrs. Goldsmith's front porch, I find comfort in looking out the window. I open the tiny latch and pull the window open an inch or two. Peace descends upon me as I reach my hand through the opening and feel the encompassing warmth. I watch in wonder as my skin and bones appear and disappear.

I wish my problems could be erased with such ease.

June 4

My fifteenth birthday starts with a moment of confusion as I wake in the spare bedroom of my dad's apartment, not quite sure where I am. As the fog of sleep clears, I sigh. I suppose this will always be the "first birthday after my parents separated," followed by "the first Thanksgiving," "the first Christmas," and on and on until we've made our way through the calendar. I glance at my phone and see texts from Charlotte and JK, both wishing me a happy birthday. I click out quick replies to both.

I hear dishes clinking from the kitchen. "Getting up sometime, birthday boy?" my dad calls.

"I'm up. Gonna grab a quick shower." I fumble in my duffle bag for clean underwear. Even though I love spending time with my dad, it's a pain in the butt to stay overnight. I have to pack clothes and remember to bring my phone charger, laptop, and all the other stuff I might need for a couple of days. At least school is out for the summer, so I don't have to worry about lugging books back and forth.

Fifteen minutes later, with wet hair, I'm sitting in front of a stack of pancakes. My dad isn't much of a cook, but it's hard to mess up pancakes made from a box mix. Actually, his are even better than Mom's because he adds cinnamon and vanilla extract to the batter.

"C'mon, you have to admit these are better than

those toaster waffles you're always eating," he says as he watches me pour syrup over the pancakes.

"Yeah, but they're awfully easy," I counter. "All you have to do is pop 'em in the toaster for two minutes and you're good to go."

"Hmm. I didn't see you make these pancakes."

"I did the important part!" I smile as I hold up the syrup bottle.

My dad chuckles. "Well, as soon as you get those polished off, we can run by the DMV to get your permit. You're all studied up, right?"

All studied up is an understatement. If I had studied as hard for schoolwork as I did for passing my driver's permit test, I'd be a straight-A student. I don't need the window's help for this subject.

I make quick work of the pancakes, run a toothbrush over my teeth, and I'm ready to go. I don't even bother to take the study booklet with me, not that I could have anyway since it was one of the things I had forgotten back home. It lay on my nightstand, full of dog-eared pages and sticky notes on sections for recognizing road signs and when to use your turn signals and the ever-important braking distances— one hundred and thirty-two feet for a car traveling sixty miles per hour. There will be twenty-five multiple choice questions, and I need twenty correct to pass the test.

Forty-five minutes later, I'm a card-carrying permit driver. I got the first twenty questions correct and didn't even have to answer the last five. The computer screen showed CONGRATULATIONS in big, green letters. The next thing I know, I'm walking out the DMV with my permit clutched in one hand and an ear-to-ear grin on my face. I fist bump my dad and practically dance to the car.

What I was not prepared for was what happened next.

"Here you go." My dad tosses me the set of car keys. I promptly drop them to the pavement and then fumble to pick them up.

"I hope you drive better than you catch," my dad says. "Should I be worried?"

"No, I'm good," I stammer, my heart pounding in my chest. I'm about to get behind the wheel of a car for the first time. True, it's the Blue Bomb, but it's still a car.

I sit through my dad's instructions on the basics of adjusting the seat and mirrors. All set, I turn the key in the ignition and hold it there. A terrible grinding noise fills the air.

"You can let go of the key," my dad says. "The car is running."

I release my death grip on the key, and, sure enough, the old beast is rumbling, ready for me to make the next move. I try to relax and slow my breathing.

"Okay, ready to give this a shot?"

When I nod, my dad gives me instructions on how to move the gear shift to reverse. I put my foot firmly on the brake and slide the lever to the R position.

"Now, check your mirrors to make sure no one is behind you."

I check all three mirrors, adjust the rear-view mirror for a better view, then check all three mirrors again.

"Okay, now release the brake."

When I gingerly remove my foot from the brake, the car starts to back up.

"Give it a little gas."

I push on the gas pedal, and the car shoots backward.

"Not so fast!"

I switch my foot from the gas to the brake and squash the pedal to the floor. My head jerks against the back of the seat as the car comes to a stop with a squeal of tires on pavement.

My dad reaches over and puts the car into park. "That was more than a little gas."

He sees the look of panic on my face and attempts to calm me, but all I can see in my mind is the car dragging JK across the street before crashing into the azalea bush.

Hands shaking, I open the door and walk unsteadily around the car and wait for my dad to open the passenger side door. Despite his coaxing to give it another shot, I drop into the passenger seat. I stare out the window as he pulls out of the parking lot and onto the street.

"Driving takes practice," he says as he navigates the way back toward his apartment.

"Yeah," I reply glumly.

"You know, your uncle Bill failed his driver's test three times before he finally passed."

I look over at my dad. He's trying to cheer me up, but this was news to me, and I wanted to hear more. "Three times? Really?"

"Yep. The first time he failed for something called 'a dangerous action.'"

"What's that?"

"Well, he got a bit too close to a lady crossing the parking lot as he began his test. Bill said he had plenty of time to get past her, but the driving examiner had a different opinion."

"And that was it?"

"Yeah, that was it." My dad chuckles. "He didn't even get out of the parking lot."

"And what about the other two times he failed?"

"He didn't get enough points to pass."

"And the last time?"

"Got a ninety-eight," my dad said. "I guess he finally figured out he needed to practice."

My dad pulled into the parking lot of a mostly empty auto superstore and put the car in park. "Ready to give it another shot?"

"I don't know, I got off to a pretty crappy start."

"So did your uncle." He opens the car door.

I slide over and take my place behind the wheel. It takes time, but I finally get a feel for how much pressure I need on the accelerator and brake to smoothly start and stop the car. Well, relatively smoothly, anyway. Left hand turns are easy. Right hand turns take more practice, but I eventually get those as well. The final test is leaving the parking lot and putting the car onto the street.

I defer that for another day.

My dad drives to his apartment, and I grab my overnight bag. I'm sure I'm leaving something behind, but I'll be back next weekend.

"I got you something for your birthday," my dad says as he pulls into my driveway to drop me off at home. "That is usually your mom's thing, but I think I did all right."

I wait in anticipation, but he says, "I put it in your bag. You can open it later."

The thought of me opening it in front of him is too painful—for both of us—so I nod and do the "guy thing" by giving him a quick fist bump. I grab my duffle bag from the back seat and trudge into the house, unable to look back at the car as it pulls out of the driveway. If I had, my guess is my dad would be purposely looking in a different direction for the same reason I didn't look back.

"Don't leave your bag in the mudroom," my mom calls out seconds before I would've done exactly that.

"I love you, too, Mom."

She chuckles from the kitchen.

I give her a quick hug.

"How was your weekend?" she asks.

"Pretty cool." I pull my new driver's permit from my wallet and show it off proudly.

"Nice job. You and your dad practice yet?"

"Yep. Just got back from the parking lot. No street driving yet, but I'm making good progress. I've got left and right turns down."

"I'm proud of you, Brian." She gives me another hug. "And, no, I didn't forget your birthday. Presents and ice cream cake after dinner, okay?"

"I don't know, Mom. I'm trying to watch my girlish figure."

"Great! More for me," Becky yells as she comes around the corner and ducks under my arm for her own hug. She's been doing that a lot more since my dad moved out. I give her a squeeze and then head upstairs with my bag.

"And don't leave your bag in the middle of your room," my mom calls after me.

How do moms always know exactly what we are going to do before we do it?

I take a glance at the rope hanging down from the attic entrance. It's like a siren call, but I have Charlotte on my mind and make my way into my room to give her a call.

"Hey, babe," she answers on the first ring, as if she's been waiting for my call. That thought alone thrills me to the core. It doesn't hurt that she calls me "babe," either.

"How was your weekend?" I ask. "Did you manage to survive without me?"

"It was tough, but I managed. Barely. How's your dad doing?"

"He's okay, I guess. His apartment isn't too bad. It's got a big pool and a workout room."

We talk about my permit and my driving practice. Charlotte is six months older than me and has had her permit for quite a while, but she listens as I explain every left and right turn and how smooth I was on braking and accelerating. Then we settle into thirty minutes of small talk about nothing. When I think back to the first tortured phone call I had with her the day after Christmas, it amazes me how far I've come.

While we talk, I look at the card she gave me on Friday before I went to my dad's for the weekend. The card itself is nothing special, a funny one she had found with a new driver behind the wheel with a terrified parent pulling their hair out in the passenger seat. On the inside of the card, the caption reads, "I have to pay HOW MUCH for insurance???" It's what she wrote beneath the punchline that draws my attention. In purple ink, in beautiful handwriting that would put a calligrapher to shame, she wrote, "Love, Charlotte." I like the sound of that.

The card came with tickets to see a local band we like. The concert isn't until October, so that means she's planning on sticking around for a while. I liked the sound of that, too.

Dinner is steak, baked potatoes, and green beans—my favorite meal—followed up with a large slice of ice cream cake. I'm scraping the last bit of chocolate fudge with the side of my fork when my mom brings out my birthday presents. She's always leaned toward practical when it comes to gifts, so I'm not surprised to see pajama pants—which I plan to keep at my Dad's place—and a couple of new shirts. I try to look excited about the clothes, but I'm not sure I pull it off. Even Becky joins in the present giving, a first for her. She gives me a homemade card. Inside is a dozen handmade coupons.

"There's one for each month," she says proudly, anxiously watching my face for approval.

I sort through the coupons, seeing "1 free hug," "1 free room cleaning," and "1 free chore." My favorite is the last one in the pile, though. "1 free night where

I don't spy on you and Charlot kissing on the porch."

"So how long have you been spying on me and my girlfriend?" I ask. "Are you the one moving the living room curtains around?"

Becky giggles but doesn't divulge her secret hiding place, something Charlotte and I have known about for months.

It's after nine o'clock when I remember my dad had left a present for me in my duffle bag. I rummage through the bag and find a small wrapped box tucked into a corner with dirty socks. I tear off the newspaper he had used to wrap the gift and find a short note:

I know this has been a rough summer for you, for all of us, I guess. I thought you could use a present that wasn't so practical (says the guy who is going to wrap your present in an old newspaper), and this is what I came up with. You can't legally use these for a while, but they will be there waiting for you when you turn 16.

Love, Dad

Under the note is a set of car keys, not for the Blue Bomb as I had expected, but for the Honda. He's taking the old Falcon for himself, so I can have something nicer to drive. Tears well in my eyes. When he got the new car, he was like a little kid unwrapping the coolest gift under the tree. And he's giving it to me! The "first birthday after my parents separated" turned out to be a pretty decent day after all.

I sit in my dad's Honda Accord—or I guess I should call it *my* Accord—for half an hour before going to bed. I picture myself pulling up a year from now, one arm hanging out of the window as I wheel my car neatly into Charlotte's driveway. I'll hold the door for her as she gets into the car, and her long, tanned legs will swing enticingly into the passenger seat. The sunroof will be open to let in the fresh air on a beautiful summer day, not hot enough to need the air conditioning yet. We'll head out for a concert, or a picnic, or...who cares? The important thing is it will be me, Charlotte, and my new car. I lean back into the comfortable leather seat and smile. Life couldn't get any better.

June 11

Becky is at my dad's apartment for the weekend. It's a two-bedroom place, so we decided we would take turns spending the weekend with him. Becky also stays there on Wednesday nights if my dad isn't traveling for work, which he doesn't have to do often. My parents are at least trying to make this as painless as possible for us. I'm not sure if it's working, though. It's tough leaving my mom on Friday night and even tougher saying goodbye to my dad on Sunday afternoon. I cling to a futile hope they will get back together, but they're settling into their new lives.

Mom's got an interview at one of the department stores at the mall. She hasn't worked for a while, so she's resigned herself to finding any job at this point. Finances were one of the sore subjects in the marriage. With the additional cost of rent for the apartment, things aren't better in that regard.

"How do I look?" my mom asks. She's dressed in a light green blouse with dark blue dress pants and a matching jacket.

"You look great, Mom." She appears unconvinced, so I add, "you got this."

She smiles. "Well, nothing ventured, nothing gained." She fishes her car keys from her purse. I give her a thumbs up as she opens the door to the garage.

I've got the house to myself, and I've got a date with Charlotte tonight, but my afternoon is completely free, so I consider giving JK a call. It's been a while since we've seen each other, and he's usually up for an afternoon of shooting hoops in the driveway, playing video games, or hanging out. My phone is on my nightstand, so I head upstairs. I come to an abrupt halt at the top of the stairs and gasp.

The attic ladder is down.

The pine steps leading to the attic look as if they've been freshly polished. For a moment, I wonder if my mom had pulled them down to clean them, but I put that possibility out of my head. There's no chair in the hallway, and, at five foot three, she wouldn't have been able to reach the rope without it.

Possibility two is the steps fell from the hatchway because they hadn't settled into place the last time I came down. Except that doesn't make sense, either. The ladder is attached to a spring that pulls the steps back into the attic unless someone latches them, as they are now. They can't fall from the ceiling and lock themselves into place on their own.

My dad and Becky aren't home, and I sure as hell didn't do it.

I'm out of possibilities.

We did a unit on mystery stories in English this past year, and one interesting point stuck with me. Sir Arthur Conan Doyle was fond of the phrase, "When you have eliminated the impossible, whatever remains, however improbable, must be the truth." Mrs. Buellencamp said Doyle had used some variation of it in at least six of his Sherlock Holmes books.

No one in the house could lower the steps. That means I've eliminated the impossible. All that remains—and it absolutely fit the definition of improbable—is that something in the attic lowered the steps.

Anyone else would unlock the steps and let the spring pull them back into the attic, but I know this cursed attic with its strange window won't let me get away that easily.

I'm scared, but I take a deep breath and climb the stairs.

The boxes in the attic have been rearranged, shoved to one side to leave a clear path to the window, which shines against the front wall. I sit in the chair in front of the octagonal opening and, terrified by what I might see, look outside.

Mrs. Goldsmith is on her front porch.

Is this lady always outside?

Wearing a hideous red sweater with cartoon pictures of cats, she sips from a cup of coffee and scans the neighborhood. Next door, Mr. Crowley shuffles down his driveway with a handful of envelopes. He takes care to check each has a stamp before depositing them into the mailbox. He gives Mrs. Goldsmith a nod—about as friendly a gesture as I've ever seen him give—and raises the red flag to let the mail carrier know he's got outgoing mail. I watch as he lumbers halfway up the driveway and out of view.

No sign of life at either the Pollock's house or the portion of the Allen's driveway and yard I can see from the window. A hopeful thought that the window isn't going to show me anything today pops into my head, but I don't believe it for a second.

A truck rumbles down the street, slows in front of Crowley's house, shifts gears loudly, and continues down the street. Mrs. Goldsmith goes into the house but returns a short time later with a fresh cup of coffee and a magazine. I can't quite make out the cover, but it might be about the royals. She takes a sip of her coffee, glances up and down the street to see if she's missed anything, settles onto her porch swing, and dives into the magazine.

Now another car comes down the street, this time coming from the direction of the Allen's house. It slows as it passes our house, and the woman driver takes a long look at our house. Less than a minute later, the woman has returned and parks her late-model car at the curb. She checks her make-up in the rearview mirror and then gets out. I get a better look at her as she comes around the back of her car. Something about her is familiar, but I can't put my finger on it.

She clicks a button on her key fob, and her trunk pops open. She removes a sign and carries it to the front yard. When I see the sign, I realize where I've seen her before. Her face is on the billboard facing the freeway near the high school.

HELEN SCHMIDT

A HOUSE-SOLD NAME

She's with a real-estate firm, and she's using a high-heeled shoe to press one leg of a *For Sale* sign into our front yard. The second leg is in the ground, and she checks the sign to make sure it is secure. Then she deposits a handful of brochures into the container.

Across the street, Mrs. Goldsmith takes it all in with a slight smile on her lined face.

I want to confront my mom when she comes back from her interview, but I can't, of course. She would have no idea what I'm talking about, unless she's already thinking about selling the house. Even then, this could be months down the line. Hell, even years since I don't know how far into the future the window can look. My lone clue is the ugly cat sweater Mrs. Goldsmith is wearing, which tells me nothing will happen in the short term. Weather forecasts are for a hot summer. It's already getting warm, and summer won't officially start for another ten days.

* * *

"I got it!" my mom yells as she walks triumphantly through the door.

I'm planted on the couch in the living room, watching the Phillies playing the Cardinals.

Philadelphia is down by four with two innings to play, so I'm not holding out much hope for a comeback. "Great, Mom." I say, without much enthusiasm.

"It doesn't pay much, but I do get commission and there's a good chance I can move up into a management position in a year or so." She looks at me, silently imploring me to share her excitement, so I give her a hug.

"Seriously, way to go, Mom."

"What do you say we go down to Dino's for a pizza to celebrate?"

"Yeah, that would be great," I say with a big smile on my face.

She can probably see right through my fake grin but chooses to ignore it. "Let me change out of these clothes first."

"Sounds good."

The Cardinals score two more runs, putting the game completely out of reach, so I click off the television and sink into couch cushion with my eyes closed.

June 24

I call Charlotte, but she doesn't answer. I don't bother to leave a message because I figure she'll call back when she sees I called. I mow lawns to make money during the summer—it turns out girlfriends can be expensive—but it's rained the last two days, meaning mowing is off the table until the yards dry out. Becky is out to a movie and lunch with my dad and my mom is working, so I've got the house to myself. I text JK to see if he can come over. He responds with *Sorry man, can't today. I'm on my way to visit Mrs. Wilson's new grand-niece. Please rescue me! And what the hell is a grand-niece anyway?*

I turn on the television, but despite having a hundred cable channels, nothing looks good. I make a snack, remembering to clean up after myself so Mom can come home to a clean house. Still no return call from Charlotte.

I've begun to settle into my new existence. Mom works a lot during the week. She loves her new job and comes home tired but exhilarated. I've been helping more around the house, doing some of the cleaning, the occasional load of laundry, and cooking a few meals when my mom works late. I don't get too extravagant, mostly mac and cheese or grilled cheese sandwiches, but my sister doesn't complain. Charlotte helped a couple of times and the meals got a lot better. She makes a mean lasagna and her parmesan chicken pasta is better than anything I've ever had in a restaurant. Of course, I'm head over heels in love, so I'm sure I'm biased.

My dad is adjusting, too. He's even working on giving up smoking. While I was there last weekend, his small kitchen table was littered with wrappers from nicotine gum, which he chews furiously as we watch the Phillies on TV. His constant chomping is annoying, but I don't say anything because I want to support his effort to quit. We do the usual meals at the apartment—Chinese takeout on Friday night and pizza delivery on Saturday. It's all good with me, though. I don't go over there for great food.

I guess we can adjust to almost anything if we're given enough time, but I don't think I could ever get used to JK not being a part of my life. It was time for me to stop this.

Thirty minutes later I am across the street from the Wilsons' house. The place looks deserted, which it should be if JK's text was accurate. The carport is empty except for a barbeque grill and some garden tools on a pegboard.

And JK's bicycle, securely locked around one of the 4x4 supports for the carport roof. If this was a

121

spy movie, I'd pick the lock and make off with the goods. There is no need for that, though. I know JK's combination. He had set it to 1-1-1-1 because, as he put it, "no one would ever think of trying that". I glance both directions, but the intermittent rain is keeping everyone inside. I nonchalantly stroll across the street and knock on the Wilson's front door. I'm not expecting an answer, but it gives me another chance to check for anyone who might be watching. The coast looks clear, so I quickly walk into the carport and spin the dials to 1-1-1-1. The lock slides open. I put the chain into my backpack. After one more check to see if I can see anyone, I swing my leg over the bike and pedal away.

I ride at a slow pace through the light drizzle until the end of the street, then turn on the jets when I reach the corner. I want to put as much distance as I can between the bike and JK's house. If I can't control the window, at least I can make it impossible for it to hurt my friend. I pedal to the south side of town, a declining area of dilapidated houses and dingy storefronts. I dismount the bike and roll it into an alley between a pawn shop and a place advertising payday loans. I drop the bike onto a pile of trash cascading out of an overfull dumpster. I toss the bike lock into the dented metal trash bin, startling at a scurry of movement at my feet. I catch a glimpse of a long gray tail as something runs behind the dumpster. I hustle out of the alley and begin the long walk home.

I check my phone. Still no response from Charlotte.

Maybe she is busy with family stuff. Maybe her phone died because she forgot to charge it. Maybe she is somewhere without good cell coverage. Maybe, maybe, maybe—all good reasons for her to have not returned my call yet. But when you are a five dating a ten, other reasons run through your mind, reasons like she's getting tired of you or she met someone else.

I call her again, but she doesn't pick up. I text her but no response, even though the messaging app tells me she has seen my message. I go from worried to pissed off.

Finally, my phone rings. I glance down and see it's Charlotte. I consider giving her a little of her own treatment and not answer, but I finally swipe to answer.

"Yeah?"

"Hey, Brian, sorry I—"

I cut her off. "No need to apologize."

"What's wrong? You sound like you're mad."

"I'm not."

"Okay, but it sure sounds like you are."

"Look, if you don't want to return my calls and texts, that's your choice," I say, trying to keep my anger in check.

"If you'd let me explain—"

"Like I said, there's no need."

"I was in the emergency room for the past four hours, but if you don't want to hear about that, fine!"

"What? But why didn't—"

"Why didn't I what? Explain it to you?"

"Yeah, I mean..."

"I tried to, but apparently your delicate feelings were hurt when I didn't drop everything to immediately respond to your text."

There's a long period of silence. I check my phone to make sure she hasn't hung up on me, but I guess she's waiting on me to answer before going on.

"Are you okay?" I ask quietly.

"I'm fine. My mom tripped and fell down the stairs."

"Oh my God! Is she all right?"

"She has a sprained wrist and a few bruises, but they kept her under observation for a few hours to make sure she didn't have a concussion. We're home now, but we're supposed to wake her up every couple of hours to make sure she's okay."

"Look, Charlotte, I'm..." I trail off, not knowing where to take the rest of my sentence.

"You're what? Sorry for being such an ass?"

"I guess I couldn't have said it any better than that."

My contrite response breaks the ice.

"I'm sorry, too, Brian. I didn't mean to jump on you. It's been a stressful day."

Welcome to my world, I want to say, but I keep my thoughts to myself.

July 10

JK texts me around ten. With our girlfriends out of the picture for the day—Charlotte has out-of-town relatives visiting and Heather, JK's girlfriend of the month, is hiking with friends—we head to the mall to hang out. We make a couple circuits of the food court, dining on free samples before an overweight mall security guard tells us to move it along.

"What's up with that?" JK complains. "They offer us food, and we eat it, but we're doing something wrong?"

"I guess going for the third lap was too much," I say.

"Well, I don't know what he's complaining about. Look how fat that guy is. He looks like he lives in the food court."

"That's probably why he threw us out. We were cutting into his food supply."

While we stroll through the mall, JK keeps up a running commentary on everything he sees, an unaudited stream of consciousness that leaves me in stitches.

"Okay, so check this out," he says as he stops

abruptly in front of a display of bras in the lingerie store window.

"What?"

"So, we've got all these mannequins wearing bras, right?"

I nod, not getting his point.

"But none of them have arms. So, how did they put on the bras? Plus, they're all silver. Do you know any women who are silver? The whole thing doesn't make sense. I would love to ask them how many armless silver women shop in their store."

I can't argue with his logic, so I shake my head and laugh.

Two entrances down, we arrive at the video game store. With nothing but time on our hands, we spend the next forty-five minutes trying out the latest game systems. JK beats me in four straight car racing games.

"Dude, I thought you'd be better at driving by this point. I'm going to recommend the state takes away your permit."

"Hey, I am getting better. My dad let me drive on the highway last weekend."

JK peers over, clearly impressed. He's six months older than me but hasn't gotten his permit yet. He said it doesn't matter since the Wilsons won't let him drive their car anyway. I consider asking my dad if he can take JK out for a few driving lessons.

"Damn, these graphics are amazing," JK exclaims as his car crashes into a light pole in a fiery explosion. "When I graduate and am making serious cash, I'm buying a system like this."

"Good, then I won't have to spend my hard-earned money on one."

"You think I'm going to let you play on my system after a performance like that?" JK asks.

"I just need a little practice."

"Dude, that's like saying a septic tank just needs a breath mint."

I am still laughing as we leave the video store. I check my phone for the time.

"Hey, I've got to be heading home soon."

"Sure, I've just got to pick up something at the sporting goods store" JK said.

"Wait, you're actually going to buy something at the mall? Something other than food?"

"Yeah, I need to pick up a bike lock."

I stop dead in my tracks. "A what?"

"A bike lock. I don't know what happened to it. When I went out to the carport last night, it was gone. Maybe 1-1-1-1 wasn't the best combination after all."

"What about your bike?" I ask in a strained voice.

"My bike was there, just not the lock. Weird, right? I think this time I'm setting the combination to 9-9-9-9. No one would ever think of that."

I barely heard JK's last words as he walked away. All I could think was that I am helpless to stop what is coming. The window had found a way.

July 17

It's a scorcher, eighty-eight degrees by mid-morning, with humidity to match. I work up a sweat on the short walk to the end of the driveway to pick up the paper for my mom.

"Oh, those poor trees," I tease her, not for the first time, for being one of the last people on the planet who gets their day-old news printed on paper.

She ignores me by ducking behind the front page while she sips her third cup of coffee. I reach into the stack and pull out the sports page. The Phillies are wallowing in third place, dropping further each day. With football season coming up, I scan an article on the pre-season hopes for the Eagles.

Charlotte is in Florida, at the beach with her parents and little brother. She promises to send me pictures in her new bikini she assures me I will "absolutely love." I was planning to take my sister to the pool later in the afternoon, but I'm rethinking that as I contemplate the excessive heat. Visions of Charlotte's new bikini flit through my head while I lounge on the couch, listening to our ancient air conditioner rattle as it strains to keep up with the heat. A sudden thump wakes me from my stupor, and I look over at the front window and catch a glimpse of an Allen twin as he reaches into one of our bushes to retrieve a bright yellow frisbee. There's something familiar about this scene, but I can't quite put my finger on it.

Several minutes pass before my brain makes the

connections between Dustin Allen, a yellow frisbee, and JK. When the last synapse fires, I leap to my feet and run to the front window in time to see JK fly by on his bike, somersault in the air, and crash into the car Dustin is backing out of the driveway. I watch helplessly as JK's body collapses under the rear bumper, one leg crushed as a tire mashes it into the pavement. I lose sight of his body as the car careens across the street, coming to rest on top of the Pollak's azalea bush. Left in the wake of destruction is a single tennis shoe and a bloody streak.

My mom rushes into the room as I scream.

She sees the car but doesn't understand. "Brian, what happened?"

I've got no words to answer her. I crumble to my knees when my legs are no longer able to hold me upright, and then to the floor where I lay in a heap. Wracking sobs overcome me. My mom drops to her knees and wraps her arms around me, clueless as to what's going on but offering comfort. I shrug her off and rise unsteadily to my feet. I've got to go to him, to see if he's conscious, to tell him I'm sorry, that I should've done more. And if he is dying, I need to be the last person to touch him before the life drains completely away, as his body grows cold and his heart ceases pumping blood.

I already know the outcome, but I have no choice but to play it out.

I run from the house, not bothering to close the front door, and leap over the bedraggled flower bed and sprint across the yard. At the edge of the driveway, I pause to take in the scene—the car on the bush, Mrs. Goldsmith, the bike smashed against the mailbox, and one bloody shoe in the middle of the street.

"JK!" I scream, but of course there's no answer. I cross the street slowly, delaying what I already know

I'll see when I get to the other side. Halfway across, I pause to pick up the bloody shoe.

JK is going to want this. It's his favorite pair.

When I reach the Pollack's yard, my mind clears. I run to the car and dive to the ground so I can see underneath. On the other side of the car, Dustin retches, and I wonder if I'll be able to hold in my own breakfast. What's beneath the car no longer resembles JK, or even a human body. Instead, there are strips of cloth and mutilated flesh. I close my eyes, press my face to the warm grass, and weep.

So much happens in the next hour it's impossible to take it all in. Police cars, an ambulance, and two firetrucks arrive ten minutes later. Their blaring sirens draw the looky-loo neighbors from as far as three streets over. A tow truck drives into the front yard to lift the Allen's car on a chance JK is alive, although anyone who checks under the car has dismissed that possibility. My mom calls JK's foster parents. Mr. Wilson is on a business trip, but Mrs. Wilson arrives five minutes later. She's wearing two different colored shoes and can barely make it out of her car. She weeps, and my mom hugs her. Then I cry and Mrs. Wilson hugs me. Pockets of neighbors watch the whole spectacle. Their muffled conversations ask questions like: who is under the car, why is the Bingham boy crying, and were the Allen boys drunk?

I mean, how else do you run over a bush across the street when you're backing down your driveway?

Paramedics declare JK's death. The coroner arrives and does the official pronouncement. His remains are carefully placed into a body bag and loaded into the back of the ambulance When it pulls away and the neighbors finally disperse, my mom gives me a couple of pills she takes sometimes to help her sleep. Non-prescription stuff, but the combination of the pills and dealing with the day's trauma knock me out cold. I sleep from two o'clock until ten, awakening with a pounding headache and a sour taste in my mouth. I try to remember if I had thrown up, but I have no recollection. I brush my teeth, but the bitterness remains.

I check my phone. Charlotte called after four, but I slept right through her call, as well as the follow-up calls every ten minutes for the next hour. Her voicemails grow increasingly desperate with each call. I shoot her a quick text to let her know I'm okay but not available to talk. The pills and sleep have left me groggy and I'm going to need my head clear when I talk to her.

My dad has called, too, but he didn't leave a message.

There are texts from friends who know how close JK and I are...*were.*

A light comes into my doorway, and I'm filled with fear it's emanating from the attic, that it's calling me, anxious to give me a gruesome preview of another loved one dying. I peek through my bedroom door, but the hallway ceiling is dark. The light is from downstairs, and the clink of metal on china makes me wonder if my mom is having a late supper. I'm hungry myself since the last thing I had was a couple slices of cinnamon toast for breakfast.

"Hey, buddy, how are you doing?" my mom asks as I enter the kitchen. She's eating a piece of cheesecake with a graham cracker crust.

"I don't know what's in those pills, but they definitely worked."

"I checked in on you a couple of times and you were out."

"Any more of that cheesecake in the ice box?" I ask.

"Yeah, let me cut you a slice. Want cherries on it?"

I stare at the cherry juice running onto her plate, and my stomach gives a lurch as I recall the bloody path JK's body made as the car dragged him across the street. "No, the cheesecake is fine."

We sit in silence while we eat. My mom looks exhausted, and I'm still groggy from my eight-hour nap. I'm not sure how I'm going to be able to sleep tonight, but I understand why I needed to shut down this afternoon. I finish my cheesecake and grab a banana from the bowl on the counter.

"I finally got Becky down," my mom says. "She is heartbroken."

"Yeah, JK liked her. He teased her a lot, but he liked her."

"He was like another big brother."

"Yeah, like someone needs two smart ass big brothers," I say with a forced smile, thinking about how we would torment her together, but she'd save her anger for me. JK got a free pass every time.

"You going to be able to sleep tonight?"

"Maybe. Do you have any more of those pills?"

I doze for a bit, but never quite fall asleep. I'm wide awake at two in the morning, staring at the ceiling in my room, trying to think about anything but JK, but all thoughts lead back to him. I wonder if I'm in shock but can't figure out why. After all, I've known about his death for months, pretty much everything about it except the exact date. The window showed in brilliant technicolor. Nothing was left out.

Nothing.

Except there was, wasn't there?

I was there before Mrs. Allen arrived on the scene, so why hadn't I seen myself through the window? Why hadn't I seen myself walking across the street, stopping halfway across to pick up the bloody shoe? I should've been visible from the attic window, but I never saw myself make an appearance.

THE WINDOW
Where was I in the preview?

July 20

The parking lot at the funeral home is full when we arrive. My dad finally finds a spot to park on the street. I reach over and give Becky's hand a squeeze, and she breaks into tears. This is a first for her. It's mostly new to me, as well.

My grandfather—my mom's dad—passed away when I was five, and I vaguely remember going to the funeral home with my parents. Since we were family, we arrived before visiting hours. The long room was all dark shades and muted lighting. The thick carpet and curtains absorbed the noise so all I could hear was my own breathing.

The casket was at one end of the room with several splays of flowers on either side. *Beloved Father*, one read, which I learned years later was a bit of a stretch.

I approached the shiny wooden box but didn't go closer than ten feet. I stretched up on my toes and peered in, but I didn't recognize the skinny old man dressed in a charcoal gray suit that looked two sizes too big for him. My mom and grandfather hadn't gotten along, so I had only seen him a few times, and the cancer that ravaged his body had taken its toll on him before his death. What remained was a shrunken cadaver who was a total stranger to the five-year-old boy wearing uncomfortable dress shoes and a clip-on tie.

My mom cried, but it was more because of what she had missed when he was alive than for what she was losing with his death.

I cried because my mom cried, not because of the guy in the polished wooden box.

Unlike my grandfather's funeral, with a few old friends and distant relatives, the room holding JK's casket is filled to overflowing. JK was popular at school, and hundreds of kids cluster together in small groups, talking quietly as they remember their friend. Heather sobs on a small couch against the back wall, while being comforted by a group of her friends.

The casket is closed—nothing to see here, folks, so move it along—but there is a long line of mourners waiting patiently to pay their last respects to their classmate. I watch as they file past the casket, bow their head, or reach out a hand to touch the shiny wood as they pass. The Wilsons stand by the casket to greet guests, but they look uncomfortable in this role of "parents."

I wait in the line with my parents and sister. There's nothing to say, so we shuffle forward in silence. My mom helps my dad straighten his tie. I'm thankful my parents are together to support me during this time, although I'm not naïve enough to think this will change anything. When the last shovelful of dirt is tossed onto JK's grave, they will still be separated. Still, I appreciate the gesture.

I manage to keep my emotions in check. Part of that, I'm sure, is because I've been living JK's death for months. I've had plenty of time to progress through the five stages of grief—denial, anger, depression, bargaining, acceptance—although I can't say I've fully made it through that last stage.

Becky loses it as we reach the front. She sobs into my dad's chest and reaches a tiny hand out toward JK's casket. I keep it together, nodding toward the casket as I pass. I shake Mr. Wilson's hand and give Mrs. Wilson a quick hug. I'm turning away when Mrs. Wilson touches my arm. I look back toward her.

"Joseph would have wanted you to have this," she says as she presents a small wooden box.

I'm filled with so much emotion I can't breathe.

I picture JK brandishing his wand and declaring

he's one bad ass dude. And then I can't see anything but a blur through my tears. I totter, afraid my legs will no longer hold me up. My dad catches me before I fall and helps me to a nearby chair. I tuck my head down and draw in deep breaths. Around me I hear murmured voices, but none are clear enough to make out individual words.

I wish Charlotte was here.

There is a parade of cars from the funeral home to the church. We drive slowly with lights on, and a police car with flashing lights escorts the long line through the stop light on Olive Boulevard. There is silence in the car, and I stare out of the window at nothing.

The funeral is a blur. There are hymns and prayers and the minister's soothing voice trying to make sense of the senseless, but I check out through most of it. Instead, I remember JK.

It was the beginning of the second semester when JK walked into my first-grade class, his black hair long and curly on top of his head. He was wearing a Toy Story backpack over one shoulder, an instant giveaway that it was secondhand as he hung it on a hook next to a neat line of brand-new Frozen models. My teacher asked me to sit with the new kid at lunchtime. One of the second graders made a comment about his backpack, but JK just grinned.

"It's retro," he told me.

"What's that mean?" I asked.

"You know, something so old that it's coming back in style again."

"Oh," I responded, not quite getting what he meant.

"You watch, in six months everyone will be wanting a Toy Story backpack." He smiled before taking a big bite out of his peanut butter and jelly sandwich.

134

I couldn't have put into words back then what JK had, but I could now. Some people would have called it confidence, but I think a better term was acceptance. He acknowledged the cards he had been dealt in life and was happy to play out his hand with no regrets. It was an inner peace that no one could take away from him.

We were inseparable after that day. We sat together at lunch and spent recesses playing wallball, a game JK invented and never lost due to the complicated rules he created and amended at will. During the week, JK would come over to my house early. My mom would make him toast with sugar and cinnamon while he waited for me to get ready. I noticed that she always slipped something into his lunch bag, chocolate chip cookies or chips or an apple. When we walked home from school in the afternoon, she always had a snack for us. For someone so thin, JK could put away some food.

The weekends were the best. We'd ride our bikes out into what we called the country, before it was slowly replaced with subdivisions and strip malls. We'd pack snack food and juice boxes in our Toy Story backpacks. Yes, within six months I had begged my parents to find me a backpack to match JK's. My mom had found one in a secondhand shop and I wore it until the straps finally gave out at the end of third grade.

On one trip, we had pulled our bikes into the shade of some trees by a small pond. After eating a couple of bags of chips and downing lukewarm juice, JK taught me how to skip rocks across the water. My record had been five skips, but he managed to get one to bounce all the way across the pond and into the brush on the other side.

But my favorite memories of JK were probably just hanging around, shooting the bull about nothing and everything. He'd laugh at my lame jokes, but his were always funnier. One time he told me a story he claimed he had seen on the news. A man had his small baby in a car seat in the back seat when he stopped at a liquor store for a twelve-pack of beer. Forgetting his child was in the back, he had tossed the beer into the back seat, right on his head. I had gasped and asked if the baby was okay.

"Yeah, luckily it was light beer," he had responded with a straight face.

Looking at my face, he had added that he was just kidding.

Just kidding.

He insisted JK stood for Just Kidding. I'd been in enough classes with him to know his first name was Joseph, but I didn't know his middle name was Kurt until today when I read it on the program. The words swim through a mist of tears I don't think will ever stop. The closed casket mocks me from the front of the church. I wait for the closed lid to spring open and for JK to sit up, a crooked smile on his face as he yells out that he is "just kidding." But the lid remains closed as the pall bearers roll the wooden box down the aisle and into the waiting hearse.

After the funeral my dad drives through a fast food place on the way home and picks up burgers and fries because none of us have had any food. We eat them around the kitchen table, but no one finishes their meal. My dinner goes untouched as I sip on a chocolate shake. At one point, my dad leaves to return to his apartment.

July 24

I answer the door and Charlotte is there. Without saying a word, she wraps her arms around me. I cry unashamedly, my tears flowing into her hair. When I break the embrace, I look at her before giving her a soft kiss.

"Thank you," I say, woefully inadequate words for what that hug means to me.

We hug again before going up to my room to talk. She lets me do most of the talking, each word doing its part to thaw my frozen heart.

"I wish I could've been there for you." She caresses my arm as she gazes into my eyes.

"Me, too," I said, "but, I guess, in a way, you were with me."

"What do you mean?"

"Well, I don't think I would've made it through everything without thinking about you."

Now she's crying, and we hug again. I hold her tight and don't let her go for a long time.

July 28

I wake with my body aching and drenched in sweat. I'm lying on the floor of the attic, curled into a fetal position beneath the window. A single beam of light shines directly into my eyes, and I shut them against the painful brilliance. I don't remember coming up to the attic, but I vaguely recall having trouble sleeping and slipping downstairs for a couple of my mom's sleeping pills.

Maybe I'm dreaming.

Even through my closed eyelids, the light from the window penetrates. I turn my head, but even the reflection off the plywood floor causes me to flinch. Relenting, I unfold myself and rise to my feet. I don't want to look out the window, but I know I will.

Do I have a choice anymore?

Outside the window, it's full-on autumn. The trees are covered in reds and yellows. A brisk wind sends cascades of leaves tumbling from the branches and across yards in swirling pockets of color. Across the street, a woman in a thick wool sweater is walking a pair of black Labradors. I don't recognize her or the dogs. She has her head down as she walks against the wind. Her dogs are thoroughly enjoying their walk, pouncing on windblown leaves and rolling in the gathering piles.

The street in front of the Allen's driveway still bears the bloody mark. I try to avert my gaze, but I trace the mark from the driveway all the way across the street to the Pollack's front yard. The azalea bush is gone—it didn't survive the car crashing into it— and there are deep gouges in the yard from the tow truck, but it's the discolored concrete that draws my attention.

As painful as the memory of that day is, I don't want the stain to ever fade.

It's a daily reminder of my best friend.

Through the window, I watch my sister across the street, sitting on the porch swing with Adam Pollock. Apparently, things are progressing in that little romance, although they're as far apart from each other as the swing will allow. Adam's hands wave nervously in the air as he talks. Becky is the calm one, watching him with a slight smile on her face. She's wearing a coat, but only her left arm is in a sleeve. The other sleeve is hanging loosely.

Mrs. Goldsmith gives them a look out of the corner of her eye as she walks down her driveway to check the mailbox. She peers in the metal box but comes up empty. Pausing to light a cigarette, she cups her hand to keep the wind from the lighter, all the while watching what might be happening on the porch swing next door. Cigarette lit, she ambles back up the driveway, with her head turned to keep an eye on Becky and Adam.

Something purple moving in the gutter in front of Mr. Crowley's mailbox catches my eye. I squint to make out a piece of knotted cloth. As the stiff breeze rolls it in front of my house, I see it more clearly, and my heart catches in my throat.

It's a purple scrunchie.

I lose sight of the scrunchie as the wind pushes it past our mailbox and in front of the Allen's house. I scan the rest of my field of view, hoping to get an idea of what I'm supposed to see, but there's nothing but blowing leaves.

"What are you doing in the attic?"

Becky's voice startles me, and I slip off my chair and fall to the floor. She laughs but cuts it off quickly and puts a hand over her mouth.

"It's okay to laugh, Becky."

"No, it isn't. Not after JK..." She breaks into tears.

I get up from the floor and wrap my arms around her in a tight hug. "He loved you," I tell her through my own tears.

When I finally let go, Becky sinks into the chair. I slide to the floor next to her, and she puts her head on my shoulder.

"I'm going to miss him," she says.

"Me, too. He was my best friend."

"Even a better friend than Charlotte?"

"Yeah, but not as good a kisser," I say, eliciting

a smile from her.

We sit for a few minutes, thinking about JK and our loss.

Becky finally breaks the silence. "You never did answer my question."

"What question?"

"What are you doing in the attic?"

"I'm looking..." I start but trail off. My next words will be pointless.

"Looking at what? Dusty boxes?"

"I'm looking to see if there are pictures of JK up here."

"Oh, want me to help?"

"No, I'll head down in a minute."

Becky gets up from the chair. "Okay, I'm headed down, too. This place is spooky in the dark."

I bite my lip. The light shining through the window illuminates every corner of the attic, but of course Becky can't see the window, so the room remains dark to her. She picks her way around piles of boxes as she moves toward the hatchway. I see her head for a moment as she comes around the last stack. She's at the opening when she jerks forward. I watch in horror as she falls through the hatchway.

A crunch sounds, followed by a scream.

By the time I reach the bottom of the attic stairs, Becky's left arm is already swelling. She's holding it to her chest and bawling her eyes out. I'm about to go to my room to get my cell phone to call 9-1-1 when the garage door opens.

"Mom!" I cry out at the top of my lungs.

My mom flies up the stairs two steps at a time and takes in the scene in an instant. She helps Becky to her feet and walks her carefully down the stairs and into her car. In twenty minutes, we're entering the emergency room. A nurse assists my sister into a wheelchair and rolls her down the hall and out of sight, with my mom close at her heels.

I plop down in a chair to wait. And wait. And wait.

Sometime later, my dad rushes into the emergency room, with a look of deep concern on his face. He sees me and hustles over.

"What happened? How is Becky? Your mom's text said Becky had hurt herself and you were all in the emergency room."

I explain that Becky fell down the stairs—I purposefully omit the key fact it was the attic stairs—and landed on her arm. I add that I haven't heard anything since the nurse took her away about an hour earlier.

My dad checks for an update at the information desk, but they don't know any more than I do. They promise to let us know as soon as they learn something. So now we both wait.

"They're probably taking x-rays," my dad says, while checking his cell phone for messages. "Still nothing from your mom."

Another hour passes before my mom makes an appearance.

"It's a clean break," she explains. "They're putting on a cast. She'll be fine. She's actually excited she'll have the cast when school starts because she wants everyone to sign it."

I heave a sigh of relief.

"Well, I could sure use a cigarette," my mom says, already turning and heading for the exit. She stops when my dad doesn't follow her. She tilts her head to one side as if puzzled.

"I'm good," he tells her.

"Really?"

"Yeah, Monday will be a month since I quit."

My mom nods. "Good for you," she says sincerely. "Good for you." She leaves us in the waiting room while she moves toward the door, fumbling in her purse for her cigarettes.

With all the commotion of Becky getting a cast on her arm—a bright lime green one that extends from her wrist to her elbow—and JK's death, the subject of the attic steps doesn't come up. I'm prepared to stick with my story about looking for pictures of JK in the boxed photo albums in the attic, but I'm not sure if my mom will buy the story. She has to have noticed how much time I spend up there, although that's pretty self-centered of me since she's also dealing with a separation, a new job, and single-parenting two kids.

August 2

I'm lying in my bean bag chair, and I have a book open, but I can't concentrate. I've read the last paragraph three times and can't remember what it says. The blurred words are swimming across my eyes when Becky slips quietly into my room.

"What's up, Becky? How's your arm?"

"It doesn't hurt much, but it's hard to get comfortable in my bed with this stupid thing."

She sits on the side of my bed and stares at me for a long time without speaking. I'm about to say something when she breaks the silence.

"It wasn't an accident, Brian."

I look at her carefully. Her face tells me she has thought carefully about what she's about to say.

"What do you mean?" I ask.

"It wasn't an accident," she repeats. "I didn't fall down the steps."

"What do you mean? What do you think happened?"

"Someone pushed me."

I recall her fall, that sudden jerk forward. "Are you sure you didn't trip on something, like a box?"

"I'm sure."

"There's a lot of—"

"I didn't trip. I was pushed."

I consider that a moment when she clutches my arm.

"Promise me something, Brian." She waits until she's sure I'm listening. "Promise me you'll stay out of the attic."

I don't understand what happened to Becky that day. I prefer to think she caught her foot on the corner of a box and fell through the opening. It was dark, at least to her, without the benefit of the light streaming through the window. That explanation is plausible, but it also allows me to avoid having to think about the other option, that the window had something to do with it. Because something that can push an eight-year-old girl down a flight of stairs might be capable of doing far worse.

August 26

"**B**rian, up and at 'em," my mom calls up the stairs.

I lift my head and glance at the clock—6:45. I groan and lay back in the softness of my pillow.

It's the first day of my sophomore year. A year ago, I'd been scared to make the leap from middle school to high school, from being the top dog to a lowly freshman. Now I have a year under my belt, and I have a steady girlfriend. Life should be looking up, but instead I'm filled with a sense of dread.

I shower and pull on a pair of jeans and a faded T-shirt. My sock drawer is empty. I'm sure there are clean ones in the laundry room, but I give the ones at the end of my bed a quick sniff test and decide they're good for another day of wear.

Another glance at the clock. I have twenty-five minutes until I need to be at the bus stop, which is plenty of time for a glass of juice and a couple of toaster waffles.

Down the hall, Becky sings off-key as she gets ready for school. She doesn't need to leave for more than an hour, but she's excited to get the school year started. I'm sure her lime green cast has something to do with that.

I scoop up a handful of pens and a couple new notebooks and drop them into my tattered backpack. There's a small rip in one side, but it should be good for another year.

As I pass under the attic, a line of light shines

through where the hatchway isn't quite closed. I shudder as the image of a purple scrunchie being blown down the gutter flashes through my mind. I think about the attic as I ride the bus to school.

"There's my guy," Charlotte says as I approach her locker. She flashes me a smile and gives me a quick hug.

"Get a room!" someone quips from across the hall.

Charlotte smiles, but I've got too much stuff on my mind to reciprocate.

"Anything wrong?" she asks.

"No, just tired, I guess."

I am tired, but that doesn't have anything to do with my sour mood. It's the sight of Charlotte's scrunchie, her favorite purple one, holding her long hair in a ponytail. Is it the one I saw through the attic window?

"You still coming over tonight?" she asks.

"What? Um, sure," I mutter, picturing that scrunchie again, Becky falling from the attic, and JK being dragged under the car, and I wonder if there's something worse in store for Charlotte.

"You sure you're okay?"

"Yeah, gotta get to class. I'll see you at lunch."

I walk away quickly, anxious for the conversation to be over, afraid of what I might say.

I stumble through the rest of the day. New schedule, new classes, and new teachers all go by in a blur. I skip lunch and text Charlotte that I need to meet with a teacher. I hate lying, but I've been doing it for months. I spend the thirty minutes of free time in the back gym, the one nobody uses except for the wrestling team, who won't start practice for another two months. Oblivious to the rancid odor of the sweat-stained mats, I sit with my back against the wall with my eyes closed, but I'm far from sleep.

September 17

I'm twirling the dial to the combination lock when I'm pushed into the metal face of my locker. My backpack slides off my shoulder, and something cracks when it hits the floor. I whirl around and see Hank Jackson walking down the hall, laughing with two of his buddies.

"Hey, asshole!" I yell at his back.

He turns, with a look of surprise on his face.

"You'd better hope you weren't talking to me," Hank says as he comes back down the hall in my direction.

"Yeah, I'm definitely talking to you, asshole."

Another look of surprise on his face. A small crowd gathers. Mr. Siegfried, the chemistry teacher, pokes his head out of his room halfway down the hall.

"What's your problem, Bingham?"

"You shove me into my locker and it's my problem?"

"I should have kicked your ass back in middle school when I had the chance. You got lucky your little buddy JK was there that day."

I ball my fists at the mention of JK but freeze at the next words out of Hank's mouth.

"You know, your dumbass friend might be alive if he had taken his beating instead of taking off on his bike."

My jaw drops. "You were there that day?".

"Saw the whole thing from the end of the street," Hank says.

That explains everything. JK had been trying to outrun Hank when he rode by my house that day.

"You could hear his head hit that car from half a block away." Hank laughs. "It was like the sound of a cockroach under my boot."

Without warning, I launch at him. He doesn't

146

even get a hand up as I crash into him, and we tumble to the floor. For a moment, I have the element of surprise on my side. I take advantage and slam a fist into the side of his head. My finger snaps as it crunches into his cheekbone. I don't care and throw another punch. This one lands on his chin. Two more fists land in quick succession. The pain in my finger is excruciating, but I'm ready to go again before I'm grabbed underneath my arms and dragged off him. Mr. Siegfried and another teacher haul me to my feet and pull me backward.

Hank lies stunned on the floor.

I stare down at him. "That was for JK, you son of a bitch!" I shake my fist in rage, spraying droplets of blood. It must be his because I escaped without a scratch.

Then I look down at my throbbing right hand and see my index finger jutting out at an odd angle.

"Well, so much for being untouched."

I get a week of detention, which isn't as bad a punishment as I could have received. I also get sent home for the rest of the day, giving me time to heal my finger. It took less than an hour with the window's help. After the magic fog did its trick, you'd never know I had broken it.

What was much slower to heal was the feeling of helplessness that ate at me every waking hour.

I manage to rise every morning and make it through each day, but it's all pretend. I must be a pretty good actor because, besides Charlotte, nobody notices I'm going through the motions.

Becky is busy with fourth grade and the newfound celebrity status her cast has brought her. I wonder what she told her friends about the broken arm. I'm sure it was a different story than the one she had told me. Even gullible fourth graders won't buy some bullshit about someone (*something*) pushing her down a flight of steps. I've noticed Becky won't walk directly under the attic hatchway when she goes to her bedroom. She scoots to one side of the hallway and clutches her arm as she passes. After a couple of weeks, the lime green cast is old news, and she settles into fractions, state history, and the distraction of the new boy in class who has all the girls giggling for no reason.

My mom is also distracted. She's loving her job, and the move to management came months earlier than she had expected. The new role requires more hours, so I'm doing a lot of the cooking when she works late. It's mostly reheating casseroles and other meals she prepares ahead of time on the weekends. On those nights she's home, she sits at the kitchen table hunched over her laptop, with a smoldering cigarette dangling from her lips and one eye squinting through the rising smoke as she scans inventory and sales reports. She's enthusiastic about her newfound independence, but I catch a look of worry as she sorts through the bills.

I see my dad every other weekend. He has completely kicked his smoking habit, which couldn't have been easy for him after so many years of lighting up. Occasionally, he reaches for the non-existent pack of cigarettes in his pocket. He smiles and shakes his head when he catches himself doing it. Since the separation, he's packed on a few pounds, probably a combination of quitting smoking and his less-than-healthy diet of take-out food. He has a frying pan, a saucepan, and a couple of cooking utensils, but they don't often see the light of day. On Friday nights when I visit, we usually go to the local sports bar and grill for dinner. We chow down on burgers and catch up while we watch a baseball game on one of the big screen televisions. On Saturdays, we go for a drive, with me in the driver's seat of the Blue Bomb, and stop at a restaurant to bring home take-out, usually Chinese or pizza. Sometimes, my dad picks me up at the house and we leave the old Falcon and take the Honda for the weekend. I can tell by the way my dad looks at the car that he misses it, so I make sure he gets time behind the steering wheel, too.

Things with Charlotte are fine, but there's something off there, too. I catch her looking at me sometimes, with her head cocked slightly to one side as if she's trying to find the right angle to see what's wrong. We go out, we have fun, we laugh, and we make out whenever we can, but something isn't quite right. She doesn't know what it is, but I do.

October 11

Becky and my dad left yesterday for Disney World. Six days and four parks on a dad-and-daughter getaway with a hundred thousand other parents and children, all with the same great idea for celebrating fall break. I was invited, too, but I begged off, claiming I wanted to use the time to catch up on my studying. I added that it would be a great bonding experience for them. I don't think my dad bought either argument, but he didn't press me.

I have no plans to pick up a book during my week of freedom, though. Instead, with my sister gone and my mom working most of the time, I spend my free time in the attic.

I stare out of the window for hours, looking for a sign or image that will show me things are going to be okay. But there's nothing. The street is clear. The curtains in Mrs. Goldsmith's front window are closed, and I wonder if she's out of town for the day. She's got kids that live on the other side of the state, so maybe she's visiting them. The view is even emptier without her. I wonder if she puts another neighbor in charge of checking up on the neighborhood when she's not home. Well, no need to worry, Mrs. Goldsmith, old Brian is on duty and checking things out in your absence.

I'm about to abandon my vigil and head to the kitchen for a sandwich when a faint rumbling sound comes up the street. I recognize the car immediately as it enters my field of view, a dark blue Camaro with a big Confederate flag on the hood. Hank Jackson is behind the wheel, with one leather-clad arm dangling out of the window. The car slows as it passes in front of my house, and Hank raises his hand and extends his middle finger in my direction. He can't see me, but I duck back from the window into the shadows of the attic anyway. As the car accelerates with a roar and screech of rubber on concrete, I catch a glimpse of a purple cloth flapping from the rear bumper.

October 18

I skip the first day of school after fall break. I ignore the "are you lost?" and "where are you going, man?" comments from the Allen twins as I walk past the bus stop and keep going. There's no way I can go to school today, or ever again. JK died on my watch. I can't let the same thing happen to Charlotte.

I walk to the park over on Watson street and collapse onto a bench, too mentally exhausted to go farther. I used to take my sister to this park. It was her favorite because she loved the swings here. "Push me higher, Brian," she would yell, pumping her legs as she climbed higher and higher before letting go and leaping to an awkward landing, tumbling and rolling to a stop. It will be a while before she can swing again because of that ugly green cast. Thinking about the cast makes me angry. Her broken arm is on me, too, isn't it? Am I to blame for it all? Could I have prevented everything if I had never looked out of that damn window? What terrifies me is I'm not sure it's going to end.

The image of that purple cloth on Hank's bumper is seared into my brain. Was the window telling me it had something in store for Charlotte? I can't afford to wait and find out. It's time to take action. Something has to go, either the window or me.

A plan forms in my mind as I sit on the bench. Even though the weather is perfect, with school back in session, the park is empty, so I have plenty of time to think it through. Several things are clear.

The window isn't going to stop without me doing something about it. Therefore, the window must be destroyed. With that basic premise, the plan becomes straightforward. Becky is at school. My mom is at work. The house is empty, so now is the time to act.

I return home, approaching from the street behind our house and letting myself into the back door; I don't need Mrs. Goldsmith's prying eyes giving me away. I enter the garage and go to the neatly arranged wall of tools. I don't immediately see what I'm looking for and consider another alternative, but then I spot it leaning against the wall by the leaf blower—the sledgehammer my father bought to break up the concrete on our back patio two summers ago. My mom had teased him about over-compensating by buying the biggest hammer he could find. I didn't understand the joke at the time, but I remember my dad's hearty laugh like it was yesterday.

The sledgehammer is heavy. I take a few short practice swings and nod. It will do the job.

The hatchway to the attic sticks when I try to pull it down. I tug several times, pulling harder each time, but it won't budge. I put all my weight on the rope, and it opens begrudgingly with a loud squeak of rusty hinges. I extend the ladder and flip the latch to lock it in place. Taking a deep breath, I start the climb, resting the heavy sledgehammer on each rung as I pull myself up.

The attic is dark. When I try to turn on the light, the string snaps off in my hand. I reach up and pull on the metal chain to light the bulb. It illuminates in a bright flash of light and then burns out. I laugh. My nervous cackle borders on hysteria.

"You're not going to make this easy for me, are you?" I ask in the general direction of the window. Remembering my sister's fall, I make my way carefully to the hatchway. I descend the ladder, keeping a firm grip on each rung until I reach the floor safely. Downstairs, I rummage through the pantry until I come up with a hundred-watt bulb. "This should do the trick."

When I return upstairs, I'm not surprised to find the attic steps have retracted into the ceiling . I tug them down and latch them into place, and then I climb back into the dark room. I trip over a box and fall to the floor. I'm certain the box wasn't there when I went downstairs to find the lightbulb, but this doesn't lessen my determination to do what must be done. I replace the bulb, which I managed not to break, and it stays lit when I pull on the metal chain.

I approach the window, with the heavy sledgehammer hidden behind one leg. The view from the window is swirling gray with tiny spots of light, like sparkling gems hidden out of sight. I stare at the undulating cloud. That cloud doesn't appear threatening, so there's no reason for me to do it any harm.

But that's not true. I've seen what the window can do. Images of my sister's lime-green cast and JK's bloody streak flash through my mind.

I pull the sledgehammer from behind me and grasp it with two hands.

All the hitting lessons through the years, from T-ball to select baseball coaches, flood into my mind.

"Eye on the ball."

"Firm front side."

"Back foot on your toe."

"Head in the middle of your feet."

I step to within striking distance of the window, position my feet, balance, and prepare to turn my hips to generate the maximum rotational torque. I set my sight on the center of the octagon and visualize the explosion of glass as the heavy metal head smashes into the window.

Muscle memory takes over as I pull the sledgehammer back and start my swing.

The view from the window changes.

The fog clears to show an image of Charlotte. Her dazzling smile and the twinkle in her blue eyes are perfectly captured in the octagon. Her eyes widen as I swing and the hammerhead follows its course toward the window.

I try to stop my swing, but the momentum is too great. All I manage to do is redirect the sledgehammer away from the window and into the drywall surrounding the polished octagonal frame. The hammer crashes through the wallboard and into a solid two by six. The vibration shakes my body. The sledgehammer drops from my hands and thuds onto the plywood floor, narrowly missing my foot.

The image of Charlotte winks and silently mocks me.

I sag against the wall. Drywall dust settles into my hair as I sink to the floor.

The window returns to swirling fog.

I don't try again. As much as I want to smash the window into tiny shards of glass, I let the sledgehammer lie on the floor in a pile of drywall fragments. I don't think my lack of bravery is the deciding factor. Babe Ruth himself could've swung that hammer directly into the middle of the window and it would likely have bounced right off.

I turn off the light and slink down the attic stairs to my room, feeling hopeless.

Charlotte and I are supposed to go to a movie tonight, but she bails on me. The reason is what scares me.

"I'm sorry, Brian, but I'm not going to be able to make it tonight," she says when I answer the phone.

"Something wrong?"

"Yeah, I've got the worst headache I've ever had

in my life."

"My mom gets migraines sometimes," I say, "and she has to—"

"This isn't a migraine," she interrupts. "I was sitting in English and it felt as though someone hit me in the head with a hammer."

She continues, but I don't hear anything past "hammer." I picture Charlotte's class schedule in my mind. She has period four English from eleven-thirty to twelve-twenty. At that time, I was attempting to smash the crap out of the window.

Ice water runs through my veins.

It was me. I did this.

And the window wants me to know it.

October 19

I wake from a dream of the Allens' car perched on top of that azalea bush. I'm running in slow motion across the Pollack's yard. I throw myself to the ground, look under the car at a bloody scalp, and start to scream out JK's name, but then I see the purple scrunchie holding the ponytail. The dream fades, except for that purple scrunchie. I can't get that image out of my head.

When I saw the vision of JK dying through the window, I didn't do enough, and now my friend is gone. I can't make that same mistake with Charlotte. That purple scrunchie may not have anything to do with her, but I refuse to take that chance. I can't lose her, too.

And to prevent that, I have to do just that—lose her.

October 25

The day is pleasantly warm for the end of October. What I'm about to do terrifies me, though, and I shiver. I've never felt about someone the way

I do about Charlotte. I reach for her doorbell, but I can't quite work up the nerve to push the button. For a long moment, I consider changing my mind, but I steel myself to the task at hand and press it. Inside the house, the chime sounds.

She opens the door, and my breath catches in my throat as she pulls her hair up on top of her head and secures it with a purple scrunchie.

She smiles when she sees me. "Hey, Brian. I wasn't expecting you for another hour. C'mon in."

I walk into her living room. The air-conditioning raises goosebumps on my arms. I look around, thinking of all the times I stole a kiss from her while her parents were in the next room and her little brother Charlie wasn't peeking his head out from behind the couch.

"Is something wrong?" she asks, eyeing me with a slight tilt of her head.

I freeze, not quite sure how to proceed. JK would've told me to grow a pair and dive in, but he's no longer here to provide his sage advice. I know what I need to do, but my heart is holding out until the last minute.

"This is hard to say," I stammer out before freezing again.

She remains silent, looking into my eyes.

I almost lose my nerve under her steady gaze but plow ahead. "I've loved going out with you. I hope you know that."

Still no response from her other than one raised eyebrow. I was hoping for...for what? A fight to make what I must do easier?

"It's just that..." I trail off, silently pleading for her to help with this.

She doesn't.

Taking a deep breath, I get it out. "I can't see you anymore."

There, it's done. Except, it isn't.

Charlotte crosses her arms over her chest and stares at me before saying, "So that's it, huh? No explanation, just 'I can't see you anymore'?"

We are at a place I don't want to be. I can't explain why I'm breaking up without sounding like a lunatic. And I can't back out now, although there's nothing I'd rather do more. Visions of looking under that car and seeing her unrecognizable face covered in blood, the purple scrunchie taunting me from the top of her head, push me forward.

"That's it. I can't see you anymore."

I want anger. I want tears. I want her to convince me I'm wrong, to beg me to change my mind. I get none of that.

"Okay, then," she says coolly.

There's nothing to do but leave. I consider giving her a hug, but I'm not sure she will accept it. She doesn't move as I step around her. I turn around at the door, hoping for something, anything. Charlotte continues to stare at the space I had occupied a few moments earlier.

I open the door and walk onto the porch, feeling as though I'm leaving the best part of my life behind me.

That walk home feels like a thousand miles. I recall everything I've lost this year—my parents' marriage, my best friend, and now Charlotte, who went from a pleasant dream to an incredible reality to an unbearable nightmare.

Put all of that together and it's too much shit for a fifteen-year-old kid to take.

October 26

I stare at my bedroom ceiling, tracing a hairline crack from the light fixture to the wall. I don't remember that crack being there before, and I wonder if I might have created it when I slammed the sledgehammer against the attic wall. It's another cruel reminder of the window's control over me.

I check my phone, not expecting a text from Charlotte but hoping anyway. There's a message from my dad, a reminder he's picking me up early on Friday, but nothing else.

The breakup with Charlotte has sucked all the energy out of me. I want to curl up in a ball and die. Instead, I trace the crack in the ceiling over and over until I fall into a fitful sleep.

When I wake, I'm in front of the window.

Am I awake or is this a dream?

As I look out the window, I notice Charlotte. She's standing in front of my house, staring directly at the window. Can she see it? Can she see me? She locks her gaze on me, and I know she can. She smiles. Her teeth are dazzling white in the sunlight, and that smile tells me everything is going to be all right.

But it isn't.

A car engine emits a throaty roar. A streak of dark blue and the speeding Camaro crashes into her. Her body is thrown into the air, and her legs are crushed by the sudden impact. Her head smashes onto the hood, and blood spurts across the Confederate flag before her body sails head over feet across the top of the car. She lands like a ragdoll on the unforgiving pavement. The car careens from side to side, tires screeching, before correcting and racing down the street. Charlotte's body lies motionless. Her broken legs are splayed out awkwardly to one side.

And then everything plays in reverse. Hank's car backs down the street, sliding side to side as it reaches my driveway. Charlotte's body rises from the ground and collides with the rear of the car, tumbling over the top, crashing onto the hood in a shower of blood, and then back onto the street in front of the car. The Camaro continues to back down the street as Charlotte turns her sweet smile toward the window.

Then the car engine roars again. Charlotte turns toward the car. Suddenly, I shove her to one side as the car bears down on us. My body lifts (*I can feel my body lift*) and flips over the car onto the street.

I scream and am fully awake.

Everything is clear. The window is spelling it out for me. It's willing to spare Charlotte's life in exchange for mine. As I think back, I realize the window wanted me all along. The other things were bait to suck me in. The window needed me to feel enough pain so I would finally give in to its embrace. For a moment, I understand how people can commit suicide, feeling as if there's no other way to move forward to ease the constant pain. The window has brought me to that point. It has taken everything from me and is threatening to take more. When it comes down to it, I'm left with no choice in the matter.

As I have so many times before, I wonder how it'll feel to open the window and step out into that cloud. Will it carry me away from all the hurt, all the pain? I dream of being held and comforted and no longer having to think of my parents' separation, my breakup with Charlotte, and, most of all, JK's death. In the end, will the window show mercy when it takes me?

I inhale deeply and take in the window with its polished frame and crystal-clear panes showing a swirling cloud. I reach for the tiny clasp, unlatch the window, and pull it open. The fog seeks out my hand, surrounding it in a soothing caress. A slight scent of honeysuckle and lemon meets my nose. I lean closer, breathing in the smell of Charlotte's shampoo and remembering the softness of her hand in mine. From a distance, muted by the fog, I hear JK's voice. I can't quite make out the words, but I smile anyway because, well because JK always made me smile. And then a car door slams. From the solid *thunk*, I recognize it as the Blue Bomb. The comforting smells and sounds of a happier time in my life.

What I've lost hits me like a sucker punch. Tears well in my eyes and stream down my face, dripping and disappearing into tiny bursts of light as they hit the fog.

I lean closer into the fog. The milky cloud cools the burning tears. I inhale, taking the fog into my lungs and feel relief from the pain. With each breath of vapor, I become more relaxed. The cloud surrounds me, lifts me. If I step into the cloud, will it take away all of this? Will it be that easy?

I raise one leg and step over the wood frame, thinking I'll feel the solid roof under my foot, but instead it's like stepping onto a soft cushion. I pause on the edge of the window frame, knowing that taking another step will mean I might not be able to turn back, that I'll be leaving behind everything I've ever known. But thinking about the past brings sharp pain. With a sigh, I pull myself through the window and into the fog. It closes hungrily around me until I can no longer see back into the attic.

The fog swathes me in a blanket of velvety warm softness. The pain fades, replaced with...not exactly happiness or even peace, but with a realization the hurt will finally be over.

I close my eyes and let the cloud take me away.

* * *

I open my eyes and look back through the window. Instead of the dingy attic, I'm looking down on a church. A casket rests on a rolling cart in front of the altar where Pastor Guiney is speaking. There's a twinge of pain as I remember being in that same church looking at an identical casket bearing the broken remains of JK.

The fog thickens, easing the pain but blurring my view of the church.

When the pain recedes, the fog thins, and I see the church once again. My parents and sister are sitting in the front row. My dad looks as if he has aged twenty years overnight. He's wearing his best blue suit—the one he ironically called his wedding and funeral suit—but his tie is hanging crookedly to one side, as if he dressed this morning without much thought. It reminds me of my prom night and my bow tie that refused to lie straight. My dad has one arm around Becky's shoulders and is clasping my mother's hand. My mom keeps looking at the casket (*my casket*) and then down at her feet, as if it takes too much energy to hold her head erect for more than a few seconds. Becky keeps her gaze lowered, unable to look at the polished wooden box that will be dropped into the cold earth when the service is over. Tears stream down her face. Her shoulders shake with each heaving sob.

Relatives are scattered throughout the church. Aunt Janet and Uncle Robert—divorced for six years but sitting together today in the fourth row—and my three remaining grandparents. Cousins from my mom's side I haven't seen in years. A couple of older women from my dad's side of the family, whose names escape me. Neighbors are there, too. Mr. and Mrs. Allen and the twins, the Pollitts, the Jamesons, and, of course, Mrs. Goldsmith, who wouldn't miss a good funeral if her own life depended on it. JK's last foster parents are there. And classmates, fifty or more, the girls outnumbering the guys by two to one. None of them ever came close to the friendship I had with JK, but I shared good times with them over the years.

And then I see Charlotte, and a sharp pain stabs me in the gut. The fog grows opaque as it coalesces around me. I wait for the throbbing ache to subside and the cloud to thin once again. She's near the back, wearing a knee-length navy blue dress. She's pale, and her mascara is tear-streaked, but that doesn't change the fact she's the most beautiful girl I have ever seen. The anguish on her face is clear, and for a moment I wonder if she feels responsibility for any of this. I want to tell her that none of this is her fault, that she is a piece of a life which has gone from a peak to a valley at lightning speed, but as I reach out my arm, the cloud blinds me with cloying thickness. I can't even see my hand two inches in front of my face.

Seeing my family and friends brings back memories for each one—putting the earbuds in my sister's ears to help drown out our parents fighting, my dad's birthday present of the keys to his car, the dinner at Dino's pizza when my mom got her job, my first kiss with Charlotte, and, of course, the snowball fight, where JK and I had fought to a draw in that epic battle.

As I consider these fond recollections of my family and friends, the temperature of the fog drops. The warm comforting blanket becomes stinging pinpricks of ice, piercing my legs, my arms, and my face. With my vision blocked, I reach blindly toward the window, but the fog clamps down on my legs, pulling me back. The frigid cloud is all I feel as I stretch my hand toward where the window opening should be. Nothing. Then one of my fingertips brushes the smooth glass. Feeling to either side, I try to find the opening, seeking purchase on the polished wood frame surrounding the octagon, probing for entry but finding the window firmly closed. The icy fog tries to carry me away.

Now I understand. The window was never an escape. It was a trap.

Seeing how much pain I will inflict on the people I love, I realize this isn't the way, even if it'll be so easy to slip away in the fog.

I need to get back in, but my strength ebbs as the fog drags me away.

I think again about my family, about Charlotte, about JK. For a second, I see through the fog to the roof below my feet. I grab onto a shingle, and the rough texture tears my skin as I grip it. My toes near the edge of the roof, finding the aluminum gutter. I wedge my foot into the gutter and push toward the house. With a final effort, I punch my fist through the window, slicing my arm from my wrist all the way to my elbow. Grasping the frame with my other arm, I pull myself through the shards of glass and collapse onto the attic floor.

Blood streams from my arm and pools on the dusty floor. I hold a mutilated strip of skin in place as I try to get to my hands and knees. My head swims, and I fall to the floor, rolling onto my back. I look up as the fog reaches out for me with icy tendrils. I wave the wisps of gray away with my good arm, and the fog is sucked back through the broken glass. I smile as I realize the fog no longer holds power over me. I've won.

The octagon fades and the empty space solidifies until it becomes another part of the dusty drywall. For a moment I'm thirteen again, and the stack of boxes is a monster reaching out for me. But the monster is dead.

I call out for my mother in a raspy voice as darkness overcomes me.

EPILOGUE

One year later

"**H**i, Charlotte," I say with a small wave as I pass her in the hallway.

She favors me with her dazzling smile and a wink.

"Ahem." Ashley, my girlfriend for the past four months, pokes me playfully in the ribs with a sharp elbow.

I laugh and take her hand in mine. As I do, I sneak a look at the ragged scar running up the inside of my arm. I still see a therapist every other week. When everyone thinks you tried to commit suicide, you can't avoid extended professional help. Becky even went for a few sessions. She was the one who found me in the attic that day, bravely overcoming her fears to climb the steps when she heard me cry out for help. The doctors said I lost close to four pints of blood, a Class 3 hemorrhage. If Becky hadn't shown up when she did, the window would've won after all.

My therapist is okay, and some sessions are helpful as we work through painful issues. She thinks I'm getting better, and I am, but she'll never know everything. You see, I've never told her about the window. There's a good reason for that, of course. If I brought up a magical portal hiding in my attic that allowed me to see into the future, there's no way in hell I'll ever get out of therapy.

I understand my parents aren't getting back together, and I've made my peace with that. As the window predicted, my mom sold our house. We're in the same school district, so the new place will be fine. Becky decided she could do better than Adam Pollock, so she was okay with the move. I'm okay, too, since it's a one-story ranch with a crawl space instead of an attic.

I think about JK a lot. I grieve for him, but, like my scar, this profound loss is fading. His Kingsley Shacklebolt wand sits in a place of honor on my dresser, but I never take it out of its case. I've learned to laugh again, but it took me a long time to open myself up to the idea of a new best friend.

Eventually, I got over Charlotte. That may have been the toughest hurdle of all. Maybe you never totally get over your first love. Time will tell on that one.

As for the attic, I went back in there once more, a few days after I got released from the hospital, from the section JK would have called "the loony bin." I passed under the short rope leading to the attic a couple dozen times before I finally got the nerve to pull down the ladder. One of the pine rungs has a crack in it now from one of the overweight paramedics who had wrestled me down the steps on the way to the ambulance. Taking care to avoid that rung, I climbed up through the hatchway. I didn't turn on the light. In truth, the darkness was comforting.

I sat alone in the quiet gloom, with the sole light coming from the hallway below, staring at the shadow of unfinished drywall where an octagonal window had once been. The sledgehammer still leaned against the wall in a pile of drywall dust. After a while, I rose and picked my way around the stacks—not monsters, just boxes—until I reached the top of the steps. I took one last look around in the gloom before descending the stairs and releasing the latch.

— The End —

ABOUT THE AUTHOR

Dave is from St. Louis and has a degree in Computer Science. He is the author of The Math Kids series for middle grade readers. When he is not designing data center management software, he is usually reading, writing, or coaching elementary school math teams. He loves writing and his wife loves that he has found a hobby that doesn't cost money!
www.theMathKids.com

Enjoy these other titles!

Bloodwalker
By L.X. Cain

Lightning flashes.
Another child disappears...

Print ISBN 9781939844255
eBook ISBN 9781939844262

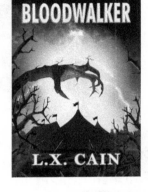

Lost Helix
By Scott Coon

Lost Helix is the key...

Print ISBN 9781939844682
eBook ISBN 9781939844699

CassaStar
By Alex J. Cavanaugh

"...calls to mind the youthful focus of
Robert Heinlein's early military sf..."
- Library Journey

To pilot the fleet's finest ship...

Print ISBN 9780981621067
eBook ISBN 9780982713938

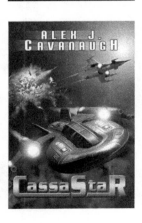

CPSIA information can be obtained
at www.ICGtesting.com
Printed in the USA
LVHW031033250121
677403LV00004B/201